POCKET

...A MODERN DAY BRITISH STORY...

'IT'S HARD TO BREAK A HABIT...

...WHEN THEY WON'T
LET YOU QUIT'

Written by... DEN LAWRENCE

Pocket is set in the real time of 2016 with all sporting events, public news and dates are 100% fact.

Characters and storyline content is a mix of twisted facts and fiction.

All characters' names are made up and are not real people.

Based on some personal true events.

#ashtag 8ighty2wo Productions Ltd

#82

CONTENTS

...CHARACTERS...

...INTRODUCTION...

CHAPTER ONE   ...THE CUP...

CHAPTER TWO   ...FAKE NOTES...

CHAPTER THREE   ...SEMI INTENTIONS...

CHAPTER FOUR   ...BLUE MONDAY...

CHAPTER FIVE   …POCKET…

CHAPTER SIX   …GOING UNDERGROUND …

CHAPTER SEVEN   …RIVERS N FLAGS…

CHAPTER EIGHT   …EUROS IN PARIS…

CHAPTER NINE   …SEA INVESTMENT…

CHAPTER TEN   …EVERYBODY'S ON THE RUN…

characters...

Joe Davies

Age 39, born... Camberwell, South London

A family man and father of two young children.

Independent, caring, creative and driven.

After years of small-time drug dealing, dead end jobs and relying on football bets, it's time to make a change.

And one for the better.

characters...

Raymond Cushion

Age 38, born... Brixton, South London

Born from a Jamaican father and a Welsh mother. Best friend to Joe for nearly 30 years. He is like the younger brother of the pair, Joe tries to keep him out of as much trouble as possible.

Cute but dopey at times. And a total fucking liability.

Football mad Ray gets by with knocking out a bit of weed, even though he probably smokes more than he gets rid of.

A real man child.

characters...

April Potter

Age 32, born... Beckton, East London

Girlfriend of Joe since 2005 and mother to their two children Denny aged 8 and Izzy, 6 years old.

Understanding and supportive, Joe's pocket rocket.

Part time cleaner and former casino worker, April is a full-time mother and homemaker, doing the school runs and running the house.

characters...

Kirsty Ball

Age 31, born... Forest Hill, South London

Girlfriend of Ray for five years, although more like a mother most of the time and best friend to April.

Kirsty works in the city for a solicitor's firm on the reception desk.

Often seen, and heard, giving boyfriend Ray a tough time.

Powerful and somewhat dramatic, not to be messed with.

characters...

Troy Deniz

Age 40, born... Croydon, South London.

Born to Turkish parents who immigrated to the UK back in the early 1970s, Troy has found his way in life.

Rising to the higher ranks on the streets and the underground world over the years.

Ruthless and sneaky, someone to avoid at all costs.

These days Troy is sitting pretty in his big home while every drug dealer on the streets is ending up running into him and having no choice to work with him or move on.

characters...

'Little' John Bridge

Age 38, born... Camberwell, South London

Nightclub owner, fixer, and former boxer and bouncer.

John gets the name 'Little' as he is six foot nine inches tall, a tower of a man.

Calmly spoken but intimidating and well known in south London, although John seems to have had his day. He has spent the last few years in his own company and is about to take work with Troy's growing business dealings, giving Little John a sense of meaning again.

characters...

Rupert Baize

Age 51, born... Brixton, South London

Former top dog on the streets and the drug world, Rupert quit the game nearly six months ago.

Getting out clean and able to enjoy the fortune he made which he started making back in the 1990s.

Well-connected and wise, he can still be very wicked.

These days Rupert has a new hobby in making music in his home studio with wife Rose, happy with the change in life.

characters...

The Lads

Jayson   Aged 26

William   Aged 24

Neil   Aged 25

Si   Aged 26

The Lads, all four are from a local estate in nearby Camberwell.

Trouble and untrustworthy, the local deep-seated urban decay. Normally found loitering the streets, street-dealing and violent, but mainly petty, crime.

All four Lads are from broken homes and have no real hope, apart from one Lad who decides not to get involved with everything the other Lads do. But sometimes, hanging around the wrong crowd can be costly.

characters...

Billy 'idol' Chalk

Age 36, born... Brighton, Sussex

Dodgy Punk rocker Billy is an acquaintance of Ray.

They met at a festival in the summer of 2013 and since then Billy drives up to London once a month with stolen goods for Ray to buy and sell on.

A scatty thief, but harmless. A sheepish rocker, and a dodgy fucker.

INTRODUCTION

JANUARY ... 2016

BRIXTON, SOUTH LONDON

39-year-old Joe, who lives with his partner of over ten years, April and their two children Denny, 8, and Izzy, 6.

Joe, along with Raymond have been ducking and diving in life for a long time now, selling anything from drugs to stolen goods.

Although Joe has now founded and set up a legit online business and wants to go legal, leaving that lifestyle behind.

Talking of which...

Troy Deniz is a top mobster and top of the hierarchy around south London these days, controlling and supplying the streets with narcotics such as cocaine.

He is helped by his right-hand man, driver, and fixer... 'Little' John Bridge who has everyone and anyone on his radar to accomplish the empire.

Ray has just struck up a dodgy deal with a contact in Brighton he normally gets knocked off electricals and jewellery from, this time the shipment is totally different to normal, and Joe is not too pleased.

But Ray also has another issue, his fiery girlfriend Kirsty.

Kirsty, best friend of April, is not happy about Ray's plans for a historic football match coming up involving his beloved team Crystal Palace, leaving him in a dilemma.

Ray's uncle Rupert, was the top dog before he retired, paving the way for Troy.

Although, you wouldn't believe that Ray and Rupert are related, one being a former criminal mastermind and the other a total fucking liability.

Rupert, under the watchful eye of his wife, Rose, who was the one who finally got Rupert to leave the underground world only months previously, may need to intervene and help Joe with his troubles.

Although Rose will not let Rupert step back into that world after finally getting out.

And getting out financially equipped, and more importantly, alive.

This is the challenging year that was... 2016.

CHAPTER ONE

THE CUP

SATURDAY, 9ᵀᴴ JANUARY 2016

10:02am…

It's a cold winter Saturday morning in south London.

Joe is at the kitchen table on his laptop, working on a project he has been creating for the last couple of years.

The project is an online betting tip service in which customers pay for picked selections by Joe to bet on and make money for themselves.

Creating a strategy along with a logo and many successful test runs, Joe is almost ready to launch his new business to the online world. After weeks of testing, he has already gathered a few customers.

Joe is desperate to get something going that doesn't involve dealing drugs and other petty criminal activity as he has a family, a missus April, and two young kids.

His phone, on the table next to his laptop, starts to ring.

'RAY CALLING'... on the phone screen.

Joe answers the phone,

"Raymondo! Where are you?" He strains to hear Ray.

Raymond is on the platform of a train station in Hampshire, football fans can be heard raucously singing in the background.

Raymond replies,

"Southampton! 3rd round of the Cup"

Ray is on his way to watch Crystal Palace take on Southampton in the yearly national FA Cup football tournament.

Joe, looking concerned, tells Ray,

"Be careful, down there."

Ray replies, sarcastically,

"Why?... coz I'm Black??"

Smiling, he leaves the train station on the south coast and strolls towards the stadium, still on the phone to Joe.

"No," Joe says. "Because it's Southampton..."

"The gaff is full of Marines, they're fucking nuts!"

"And yeah," Joe says smiling.

"Probably because you're Black too." He tells Ray who is walking out of Southampton Central train station with dozens of other Crystal Palace fans. They are being escorted by police to the stadium making sure they don't clash with Southampton FC fans.

Joe is still on the phone…

"Anyway, what are you wearing? None of that football clobber?" He asks, looking concerned.

Ray looks happy, he admires himself and confidently replies to Joe,

"Nah, all casual here bro," looking down on himself proudly.

" Got my Brixton Street Wear gear on!"

Joe, at home, looks confused and shakes his head in disbelief.

Over in Croydon…

Local mobster Troy, like Joe, is also working on his business venture... total domination.

He is sitting on a sofa in his dressing gown, gold watch, chain and rings on, stacks of cash on the table in front of him and an incredibly attractive young lady in just her underwear walking around. Little John, a club owner, minder and fixer who has known Troy for a few years, shows up at Troy's house for a meeting and an update on what Troy has in mind for his business venture.

John knocks on the door and the girl in the underwear opens it and greets him. Clearly surprising John and making him feel awkward, he gazes at the girl's legs up to her face then asks,

"Troy in?" smiling awkwardly.

The half-naked girl leads Little John upstairs, taking him to Troy who is sitting in his lounge.

Back at Joe's house...

The front door opens, Joe's partner April and their two children walk through the door coming back from Denny's football training.

Both kids run through the hallway and fly upstairs towards their bedrooms as April closes the front door. She is looking cold and weathered from standing in the elements watching Denny train with his youth football team this morning.

After closing the front door, April takes her coat off and walks towards the kitchen where Joe is sitting working on his laptop. She shouts upstairs at the children.

"KIDS, CLOTHES IN THE WASHING BASKET PLEASE"

"NOT ON THE FLOOR" she adds, as she walks into the kitchen.

She walks up to Joe, looking at the laptop screen at what Joe is working on and gives him a kiss on the cheek.

"So, is this the official logo?" April asks Joe.

Joe, unsure, mutters, "yeah."

"Looks good." April says, smiling proudly at Joe before putting the kettle on to make herself a cuppa to warm up after being out in the cold.

Over at Troy's…

Little John is sitting with Troy, having been brought a drink by the girl in the underwear. John is still looking a bit intimidated as the girl walks off and he turns to Troy.

"So, what's happening mate? How's business?" Little John asks Troy, sitting across from him.

Troy looks smug,

"Yeah, yeah. It is better than expected actually,"

"Ever since that Rupert stepped away, the world is now my oyster… well south London anyway.""

"We could have it all!" he says, looking at Little John.

"We?" John replies looking confused.

Troy leans over towards John with a serious look on his face.

"We are taking over John… Brixton, Camberwell and Peckham, for a start."

"I want every single fucker out there going through us only."

Little John nods tight lipped to agree with Troy.

A taxi pulls up outside Ray and Kirsty's…

Kirsty, Ray's girlfriend, is home from visiting family in Somerset. She pulls up in a taxi and walks through the front door of their flat calling for Ray.

"Ray… Ray?" She looks around the house then walks into the kitchen to a load of mess including dirty saucepans and plates. Even the butter has the cover off, left out from where Ray made his breakfast before rushing out to catch his train. He obviously did not tell Kirsty he was going to the football. She is now furious and gets out her phone.

Meanwhile back at Troy's…

"So, you on board?" Troy asks Little John.

Little John smiles at Troy, "I am… Boss!"

The girl in the underwear walks past and winks at John.

John awkwardly smiles and looks at Troy who is looking happy with his plan.

"Welcome to the firm." Troy says to John before they raise their drinks.

"Cheers!", they both toast to the future.

Back at Ray and Kirsty's…

A livid Kirsty calls April, Ray isn't answering his phone. He no doubt can't hear it with all the noise. It is ringing in his pocket as he sings football songs in the stadium with hundreds of Palace fans.

April, sitting reading a book at the kitchen island across from Joe on the laptop, is drinking her cup of tea, now cosy and warm when April's phone rings… 'KIRSTY CALLING'.

"Alright babe?" April answers the phone.

She pauses to listen to Kirsty.

"Ray?... No.... Nah, Joe's here at home... One sec."

April leans over to Joe,

"Do you know where Ray is? He ain't answering his phone. She don't sound happy."

While still typing away on his laptop, Joe replies,

"Yeah, he's at the football… in Southampton."

April tells Kirsty what Joe said.

"SOUTHAMPTON??" Kirsty screams down the phone looking around at the state of the kitchen.

Shortly after...

In Hampshire, the FA cup football match between Crystal Palace and Southampton has just finished. Ray is buzzing, Palace have won 2-1 and are into the next round.

But when he checks his phone and listens to a voicemail from Kirsty screaming down the phone in a rant about how messy he left the place, he knows he's probably in for an ear-bashing when he gets in.

Just when Ray thinks it can't get any worse, he turns the corner and standing in his path are three rough and quite scary looking men… Southampton FC supporters.

Ray puts his head down and walks on past, the men all stare at Ray, his heart beating as fast as the speed of sound.

Back at Joe's...

Joe is making a school project with his daughter Izzy on the living room floor when his phone rings.

Joe picks up his phone and sees a number that he doesn't recognize calling, so stands up and walks away from Izzy to answer.

"Hello" Joe says, answering the phone.

Little John is on the phone, having just left Troy's.

"Hello Joe, it's John here… We need to have a little chat."

Joe is standing there in the doorway of the living room looking confused and asks, "Why?"

"All in good time." John replies,

"Meet me outside the café at 10am tomorrow morning."

He says before hanging up.

Joe starts to look worried. He looks down at his daughter and puts his phone back in his pocket.

SUNDAY, 10th JANUARY…

It's just after 9am and Joe is up and back on the laptop working on his project. The television is on announcing the devastating news of the legendary David Bowie's death, known for most around these ways as, 'Our Brixton Boy.'. Joe is a big fan and is saddened by the news.

His cup of tea and phone are on the table next to the laptop, he knows that he must meet Little John in about 40 minutes, so will need to leave soon.

Just then Joe's phone rings.

"Raymondo… You're alive then." Joe says to Ray on answering.

Ray is in his kitchen…

"Yeah, course I am…Them silly Saints ain't got nothing on me." Ray replies with the phone pressed to his ear. He is making toast in the kitchen.

Joe smiles, amused.

"2-1, I see, into the next round."

Joe says as he looks up at the clock on his kitchen wall, knowing he must leave soon.

"Oh yeah, Kirsty rang here for you yesterday…

What have you done now??" he asks Ray.

Ray leaves the kitchen, looking back to check that he cleaned up and put everything away. He has been reminded by Joe that Kirsty was not happy yesterday and replies, "Yeah, I spoke to her; I just left the kitchen a bit untidy yesterday."

Ray walks back into the kitchen, as he has left the butter out again, and puts it back in the fridge. He then walks into the living room finishing eating his toast.

With a mouth full of toast, Ray asks Joe,

"So, what you up to today?"

"Well, I got a call yesterday, from that John Bridge or Little John, whatever his name is." Joe informs Ray.

Ray has toast in his mouth.

"Little John? Don't you mean Big John?" Ray asks with confusion.

"Yeah, but he is known as Little John. Anyway, that don't matter, what the fuck he wants is what I want to know" declares Joe.

"So, what does he want?"

Ray says again with a confused look on his face.

Joe stops what he is doing and freezes holding the phone with an even more confused look on his face, then angrier,

"WELL, I DON'T FUCKING KNOW YET... DO I??" Joe yells down the phone, undone by Ray's cluelessness.

20 minutes later, in the café…

A clock on the café wall shows 09:55. Soft music is playing on the radio and a few customers are sitting at their tables with their coffees and breakfast meals. Café owner Bleu is behind the counter when Joe walks through the door.

"Morning Bleu! One tea, two sugars to take away please" Joe says walking towards the counter.

Bleu greets Joe, smiling as ever,

"Morning Joe! How's April and the kids?

Where's Ray? Bet he loved the football result yesterday." Bleu says, while making Joe's tea.

Joe replies,

"Yeah, the family are good.

Ray is good, he's probably gone back to bed though."

Bleu hands Joe his tea which Joe pays for before leaving the café.

Just as Joe walks out of the café, a car pulls up in front of him, the passenger window drops down, John is sitting in the driver's seat.

"I HOPE THAT CUP IS FOR ME" John shouts out from the car as Joe walks towards him.

Joe stops, looks at John, looks at his tea in his hand and shakes his head, looking back up at John.

"You want sugar?" Joe asks John before turning around to go back into the café.

"Just the one sugar" Little John replies as Joe goes back into the café to get him a cup of tea before getting in Little John's car and driving off.

John is driving through the backstreets of Brixton with Joe in the passenger seat.

"So, what's this about then John?" Joe asks him.

"There is going to be a few changes" John replies.

Looking confused, Joe asks,

"With what?"

Little John, with his eyes on the road ahead responds,

"As in your supplier…

… you know, the old devil's dandruff" tapping the side of his nose with his finger and quickly looking at Joe.

Joe knows what's coming.

"Go on..." says Joe.

"You will be reporting to Troy via me from now on" John informs Joe.

Joe reluctantly declines.

"No, it's okay, I got my guy" he says, before John passes Joe the daily newspaper.

"I think you'll find he ain't around anymore."

It turns out that the night before there was a shooting nearby, with the person who was shot dying at the scene. That person was Joe's supplier who obviously wouldn't play ball with Troy and John, so John fixed the problem by arranging Joe's supplier to be shot.

Joe looks shocked as he reads the article in the newspaper and is now starting to fully understand that he is about to involve himself in something he no longer wants, and most definitely not with these two nutters.

Elsewhere, Rupert is at his home with wife Rose, sitting in his living room reading the daily newspaper.

On the front cover in bold writing...

'SHOOTING IN BRIXTON... ONE MAN DEAD'

Rose walks into the living room with a drink for Rupert, placing it beside him, she glances at what he is reading.

"Take it you see about that murder last night?"

"Good job you are away from all that now, thank God" says Rose.

Rupert pulls the newspaper from near his face, looking confused and in total shock.

"Yeah" Rupert mutters to Rose as she walks out of the room.

Back on the streets of Brixton, Little John pulls up with Joe, outside Joe's family home.

Joe, looking slightly anxious and concerned, asks John... "How the fuck do you know where I live?" He looks out the window at his house and he turns his head to look at John.

"There's not much we don't know around here, Joe" John replies calmly.

Joe gets out of the car and shuts the door.

John then tells Joe, "I will be in touch soon" before driving away.

Joe stands there not sure what to think about it as he watches John drive off. He then turns around and walks towards his front door.

While driving, having just dropped Joe off, John calls Troy.

Troy, is sitting at his desk, a half-naked girl standing behind him giving him a massage.

He answers his phone to hear John,

"Joe Davies, in the bag boss" John tells Troy.

Troy looks happy with the news, and the massage.

"Good work John, good work."

MONDAY, 12th JANUARY ...

Joe is sitting at home watching the first-round action of live 2016 snooker 'Masters' on television, when he gets another call from Little John. This time the meeting will be business.

Joe will be collecting a package from John every two weeks like clockwork.

The package will contain cocaine as before, which he will need to sell. He will also need to continue to work on his online business venture, which really needs to be a success soon.

Getting involved with the likes of Troy, or anything else dodgy, is really not what Joe needs or wants right now.

#CHAPTER TWO
FAKE NOTES

3 MONTHS LATER....

SATURDAY, 16th APRIL 2016...

Easter has been and spring is here, with longer and warmer days as the year moves on.

The World Snooker Championship has just got under way in Sheffield and Joe is at home watching the defending champion, Stuart Bingham, play his first-round match against Ali Carter. It's also Joe's birthday in a few days, he will be reaching the big forty years old.

More importantly Joe has finally launched his online business, naming it 'JD BETTING.' It has been trading for about five weeks and business is booming. Along with making cash from the cocaine packages as usual, but now only once a month, Joe's new business has earned him quite a bit already in a short space of time. He has built up a balance of around £16,000 in his bank account. Some of the money is from the drugs and Joe has had to wash it as betting winnings from his online business, but hopefully not for long. Joe can see his business growing which makes him even more determined to go legal and leave this lifestyle behind.

Elsewhere...

Crystal Palace FC have made it through all the rounds of the FA cup so far, all the way to the semi-finals. They will play Watford late next weekend on the 24th at Wembley stadium, and a win would give Palace their first cup final in 26 years.

The 24th of April is also another important date in Ray's diary.

It is the anniversary of the start of his relationship with girlfriend Kirsty, this year making it five years together.

Oh, and Kirsty doesn't like football, by the way.

Around the manor...

Troy and Little John are running town with Troy sitting pretty in his dressing gown. John is pulling the strings and has the local young street gangs doing the dirty jobs, everything is running as planned.

Except, Troy is not happy that Joe has halved his normal load to once a month rather than twice.

Troy asks Little John to keep an eye on Joe and see if he is up to anything to explain why he wouldn't need as much.

Apart from Troy and the coke, the only other thing either Joe or Ray makes anything from is when Ray's mate Billy from Brighton turns up. Normally with a load of stolen goods: laptops, watches, and other shit. This time what Billy has, is a little different though.

Ray met Billy at a festival in the summer of 2013 and with them both being off their nut, they started talking. They exchanged numbers and now Billy drives up from Sussex once a month with goods for Ray to look at. Ray can hustle a better price than Billy wants for them, so Ray normally takes most of what he has.

BRIXTON PARK...

9:08am...

Ray is up and out early, walking through the park having had to leave the house early as Kirsty is on his case about what they are doing for their anniversary night this weekend.

Kirsty herself has just left the house too, on her way to meet April. As she is marching down the road, she decides to ring Ray for another earbashing, she pulls out her phone from her handbag.

Ray is sitting in the park, he lights up a spliff and takes a couple of puffs when his phone starts ringing in his pocket.

His face drops when he pulls his phone from his pocket and sees it is Kirsty ringing him, as he has just left her.

"BABE, I'LL SORT IT" Ray yells down the phone after getting another rant from Kirsty.

Joe and April's house, 9:32am...

April has just dropped the kids off at school before meeting Kirsty on the way back home. April and Kirsty walk through the front door, April walks straight into the kitchen to make coffee. Kirsty, with a face of thunder, walks along into the living room.

"A fucking football match! Sorry, The FA cup final match" rants Kirsty.

April in the kitchen yells, "AIN'T IT THE SEMI FINALS?"

A quick response from Kirsty,

"Oh, whatever fucking match" leaving April pulling an awkward face while filling up the kettle with water from the kitchen sink.

Joe is upstairs in his makeshift office space which is in the corner of the bedroom. He has been up a couple of hours now, checking all the previous days tips he gave out, along with thank yous and other positive comments.

The online business venture is going well, Joe has gained nearly 50 customers in the last three months all paying a monthly subscription fee. Along with winning some nice bets himself, he's now taking it all very seriously.

Joe clicks onto his online banking again and logs on, the balance of £19,225 appears on the screen.

Joe has been putting as much money away as possible because he still desperately wants to get away from drug dealing with Troy and Little John.

Joe closes his laptop, nodding his head with satisfaction. He gets up to walk out of the bedroom and downstairs to where he can hear April and Kirsty talking.

April is now in the living room with Kirsty still talking about the subject of this coming weekend.

"Babe, I'm sure he will sort it" April says to Kirsty, they are both sitting on the sofa.

Joe walks down the stairs and into the living room doorway.

"I'm popping out for a bit babe… Alright Kirst?"

As he grabs his coat and starts to put it on, April gets up and walks towards Joe.

"How long is a bit?" April asks Joe while smiling and leaning in to give him a kiss.

"Not long, an hour or so" Joe replies.

Kirsty peers around April,

"AND TELL THAT PRICK, HE WANTS TO SORT THIS WEEKEND OUT" she yells from the sofa.

Joe kisses April and turns to Kirsty.

"Yes Kirsty, I will do" Joe replies with a slightly sarcastic tone.

Joe walks out the door and, closing the front door, he pulls his phone out to ring Ray.

Ray is in the café eating a full English breakfast and drinking tea when Joe rings.

"Easy brother" Ray answers the phone, sitting at a café table.

Joe has just left his house and is heading towards the high street whilst on the phone to Ray.

"Morning… got your missus at mine" Joe says to Ray.

"Yeah, I'll sort it. For fuck's sake!!" Ray replies, trying to eat his breakfast.

"Where are you?" Joe asks.

"I'm in the café" Ray replies.

Joe walks towards the high street.

"Didn't fancy breakfast at home?" asks Joe, smiling.

Ray says with a mouthful of food,

"Nah, I had to get out bruv."

Joe turns onto the high street.

"I'll be about 5 minutes" he says before putting the phone down and back in his pocket, walking into the town centre.

In the café…

Joe is now sitting across from Ray who has finished his breakfast, both are drinking a cup of tea.

"So, what did you want to speak to me about so urgent last night?" enquires Joe.

Ray replies, "I spoke to Billy last night".

Joe drinks his tea.

"What, your dodgy mate from Brighton?" asks Joe, frowning at Ray.

Ray leans forward and whispers,

"Yeah, but he has something very nice this time".

Joe leans in closer to Ray and whispers sarcastically,

"What's that then?"

Ray is unimpressed.

"£70k in fake notes, apparently good ones" he says as he looks around to make sure nobody is listening.

Joe looks slightly confused,

"What the fuck are we supposed to do with them?"

Ray leans in close to Joe,

"Wash 'em" Ray replies looking at Joe.

Joe takes a sip of his tea, pauses for a second, then asks Ray,

"How much?"

Ray is trying to convince Joe.

"I think we could get rid of them says Ray.

Joe just wants to know the details.

"How fucking much Ray?" Joe says quietly.

"Ten grand" Ray tells Joe.

"Ten?!!" Joe replies, not happy. He picks his tea back up, shaking his head.

Ray is still trying to convince Joe,

"Yeah, but that's why you're coming to meet him, you will be able to get a better price" says Ray, holding his cup of tea in his hand.

Joe shakes his head in disbelief and takes another sip of his tea before asking,

"And who is paying for these?"

Ray looks down into his cup.

"We are" he tells Joe.

Joe almost chokes on his tea when hearing Ray's response and again shakes his head in disbelief, looking around him.

Ray then changes the subject completely by asking Joe, "So, what are you doing for ya birthday?"

Joe looks at Ray with a fed-up look and says,

"Nothing mate, just another year older."

The truth being, Joe just has one thing on his mind... getting out and away from Troy, and Little John and anything else dodgy. His 40th birthday coming up is just a reminder that Joe is not where he needs to be in life.

Meanwhile, Little John is sitting in his car on his phone scrolling when he comes across an online post on Joe's betting tip business.

Scrolling on, Little John sees why Joe might be shifting only half of what he was for Troy. This discovery leads him to think Joe might be planning to part ways with drug dealing and run a proper online legal business.

"So, that's what you've been up to is it, Joe?" says John, looking at his phone.

Back at the café…

Joe is behind Ray putting his coat on as they both leave.

"Ain't you getting a bit tired of this Ray?" asks Joe as the pair walk along the high street.

"I don't get tired of making a pound note brother" replies Ray stopping and waiting for Joe to catch up.

Joe looks at Ray with a fed-up expression.

"All this meeting dodgy cunts, selling dodgy stuff. It's starting to grate on me now" says Joe.

Ray is still trying to convince Joe that all will be fine.

"It's all good, Billy is sweet, and these notes will be a good earner" Ray tells Joe.

Joe is watching Ray, trying to convince him.

"So, where are we meeting him then?" asks Joe.

"I told him to meet us at the lock up" says Ray.

Joe stops in his tracks, unimpressed by what Ray just told him.

"My lock up?" Joe asks, looking puzzled.

"Why did you tell him about my lock up? He's a dodgy cunt" Joe is now looking angry.

"Leave Bill to me. You got Troy to deal with" Ray replies.

Joe looks at Ray and then straight ahead as they both start walking again.

"Yeah, I need to talk with you about that. Not now though" says Joe as they approach his lock up.

Little John is sitting in his car...

After seeing Joe's online business, Little John sets off to see Troy to tell him what he has seen and knowing Troy, he will not be happy.

Joe and Ray arrive at Joe's lock up where keeps his dodgy business away from home. He opens the lock up door, they both walk in, and Ray shuts the door behind him.

Kirsty is still at Joe and April's house, and still moaning about Ray.

April takes the empty cups from the living room into the kitchen. Kirsty, sitting in the living room deep in thought, suddenly yells,

"THE SEMI FINAL... I'LL GIVE HIM A FUCKING SEMI" looking angry.

April in the kitchen, washing up the cups, rolls her eyes.

Back at Troy's...

Troy is sitting at his desk with Little John's phone in his hand looking at Joe's online business page. John is sitting across from him playing with a Rubiks Cube waiting for his response.

"There is something you can do John" Troy says while looking at the phone's screen.

Little John puts the Rubiks Cube down on the table in front of him. He looks at Troy, clenching his fist to crack his knuckles, smiling at Troy like he is about to get what he wants.

"No need for that yet"

"I just want you to keep an eye on Joe for me."

Troy says, while looking at Little John who is looking disappointed about not being ordered to break bones, but to do a bit of recon work instead. John nods to agree with Troy before asking,

"Is there money owed?"

"No, Joe is always upfront with cash. But that's the problem" Troy replies, deep in thought.

Little John looks confused and asks Troy,

"What do you mean Boss?"

Troy has a serious look on his face while still looking at Joe's online business on John's phone, he then looks up at Little John.

"We need to get him in our pocket before he thinks of going anywhere".

Back at the lock up...

Joe and Ray are both in Joe's lock up, Joe takes a puff of his vape and looks at Ray who is opening the shutter so Billy can drive in when he arrives.

Ray turns around and sees Joe staring at him.

"What?" asks Ray.

Joe blows out smoke still looking at Ray,

"I can't believe you gave this address" shaking his head in disappointment.

"Stop worrying"

"Billy is cool, he ain't no bother. Anyway, it's nice and quiet here" says Ray.

And just as Ray finishes speaking, loud punk music and a car engine sound comes closer.

It's Billy turning up, he pulls into Joe's lock up wheel spinning and punk music absolutely blaring from the car.

Joe shakes his head and gives Ray an unimpressed look as Billy gets out of the car and smiles at both Joe and Ray.

"Hello Ray" Billy says to Ray, still smiling.

Ray walks over to Billy standing next to his car and shakes his hand,

"Alright Bill? How ya doing mate?"

Billy looks at Joe again this time with a confused look.

"I know you" Billy says to Joe.

Joe is standing across from Billy.

"I don't think you do, mate" replies Joe, still looking unimpressed.

Billy remembers where he has seen Joe before,

"Yeah, you're that guy that does the betting."

"Fucking good as well, I see a few good winners on your site, see you got a few famous faces too."

Ray is totally confused as he has not paid any attention to what Joe has been doing, he looks at Joe, "Fuck off, what that little social media page you started?"

Joe looks at Ray and grins, "Yep" Joe says.

"Yeah, DJ or JD Betting or something ain't it?" asks Billy.

Joe takes another puff of his vape,

"Yeah mate, but we ain't here for that are we?"

Billy goes to the boot of his car, "Yeah, sorry boys." he opens the car boot.

Ray, still looking confused, turns to Joe and says…

"Why ain't you ever gave me any tips?"

Joe walks up to Ray, who is standing with Billy at the boot of the car.

"What, and have you gambling? Yeah alright!" Joe says to Ray.

Billy pulls a green-coloured bag from the boot of his car.

"Well, I got usual, few laptops and couple nice watches."

Billy then unzips the bag, "But this is what I think you want to see…"

Billy pulls a wad of banknotes out of the bag and gives a couple to Ray and Joe.

Meanwhile...

Little John is seen talking to the local gang 'The Lads' on the estate. This little firm are ruthless, proper thieving little cunts, and Little John is up to something.

At Joe and April's...

April and Kirsty are still sitting in the living room of Joe and April's flat.

Kirsty notices Joe's logo and other paperwork on the kitchen counter.

"What's this all about?" Kirsty enquires.

"It's Joe's new online business." replies April.

"What online business? Is it legal?" asks Kirsty.

"Oh yeah, totally above board, that's the whole point… Joe wants to go legal." says April.

Kirsty looks concerned.

"What about Ray, what is he gonna do if Joe goes legal?" Kirsty asks.

April smiles.

"I am sure Joe has plans for Ray somewhere babe" she tells Kirsty.

Back at Joe's lock up...

Joe is holding up a few of the banknotes, checking them out.

Ray takes a look at the notes and asks Billy,

"How much did you say again Bill?"

"£10K mate" Billy says to Ray.

Joe looks at Ray and Ray looks at Billy with a questioning look.

"I'll do you a deal, eight grand" says Billy knowing Joe and Ray are not going to pay that.

Joe looks at Billy with another unimpressed look.

Billy looks at Joe, then looks at Ray.

"OK, seven grand. They are good, they are definitely worth that" says Billy to both Joe and Ray, now seeming a bit desperate.

47

Joe puts the note to the light to check the note again,

"I'm sorry mate, but they ain't."

"I can't give you any more than a bag of sand (£1,000) max for these. That's the real value."

"And if they are do good, why don't you keep them?" asks Joe.

Hopeless looking Billy pleads,

"A grand? Ah come on Joe."

"Nah, I need to get rid of them quick, they are local, and I can't be caught with them… if you know what I mean?" says Billy while pulling his finger across his neck to say basically he would be dead if he got caught with them.

"Can't you go to at least 3 grand?" Billy pleads with Joe.

Joe puts the notes back in the bag and tells Billy,

"Look, I'll give you fifteen hundred quid for them… Final offer, take it or leave it."

Billy looks at Ray for help, Ray shrugs his shoulders to say he can't do anything.

Billy in desperation,

"Fuck sake, OK." he says, looking in the boot of his car.

"And what about the laptops and watches?" Billy asks, extremely disappointed.

"Nothing to do with me" says Joe.

Ray intervenes, "Yeah I'll sort that out Bill, no drama."

Meanwhile…

Troy is down the local snooker hall. He is getting coached by a former professional snooker player once a week for a couple of hours.

Ex-professional, Mr King has been coaching Troy for the last year to improve Troy's game.

At the snooker table…

Troy is about to take on a long blue ball into the bottom corner pocket when his phone rings. It's Little John calling.

"Sorry Mr King, I need to take this call." He picks up the phone to answer it.

"The Lads are ready Boss" John tells Troy.

"Good work John" Troy replies before putting the phone down and getting down to take his shot. He sinks the blue ball into the pocket, smiling at Mr King who is watching over him.

Joe's lock up...

Billy gets in his car and starts to drive off before yelling out the car window,

"NICE DOING BUSINESS WITH YOU BOYS."

He drives away with music blaring again.

Ray and Joe watch Bill drive off before closing the shutter back down.

"See, weren't that bad, was it? You got a good deal there."

"You think they are good copies?" asks Ray.

Joe replies, "Luckily, yeah. As good as the real thing."

"Could of give a bit more to be fair." Ray says to Joe.

Joe looks puzzled,

"Do what?... More??"

"I tell ya what… call him back and offer him more then. But you're paying it." Joe says as they both leave the lock up.

Ray walks behind Joe, "No, no, ya alright" says Ray before closing the lock up door and following Joe down the road.

Brixton High Street…

Joe and Ray are walking down the road when Joe turns to Ray and asks,

"So, what have you done now then?"

Ray turns his head towards Joe as the pair walk.

"What?"

"Kirsty" replies Joe.

"Oh that… Well, I have sort of double booked Sunday."

"Palace are playing in the FA cup semi-final, and it's also mine and Kirsty's anniversary" Ray tells Joe.

Joe smiles.

"So, what you got booked for the anniversary?" asks Joe.

"Nothing yet" replies Ray.

"Well, you ain't double booked then, are you?" Joe says, smiling at Ray as the pair of them walk back down the high street.

Ray is still intrigued by Joe's new business venture.

"So, how much you made so far?" he asks.

Joe replies,

"JD Betting? About ten grand in the last two months."

"Fucking hell bruv, why don't I know about this?" asks Ray, shocked.

Joe looks at Ray.

"I don't know. I told you months ago. Maybe you're too busy smoking weed and playing with your dodgy mate from Brighton" he says to Ray.

Ray, not looking happy, puts his head down.

Joe then looks at Ray.

"So, I take it you already got the tickets for the match?" asks Joe.

Ray looks sorry for himself,

"Yeah, I bought them the first day they went on sale last month. Thought it would be a good idea for a day out."

Joe looks confused,

"What, for an anniversary?"

"Yeah, I'll have to remember to take April to a football match on our next date" says Joe sarcastically.

"Ray, the girls don't even like football! What was you thinking?"

Ray responds, looking excited,

"Bro… It's the FA cup semi-finals!"

"Anyway, what did you want to talk to me about Troy then?" Ray asks Joe.

Joe looks straight ahead as they both walk.

"I'm quitting" he says.

"What's Troy say?" asks Ray, looking surprised.

Joe replies,

"He don't know… yet. I'm planning on telling him in the next couple days."

Ray has a realisation,

"So, what am I gonna do then?" he says with a worried look on his face.

"You always got Billy" Joe says, smiling.

Ray looks unimpressed.

"Haha… Yeah, you're funny ain't ya? You seriously cutting ties with Troy and that bit of work?" Ray asks Joe again.

Joe drops the smile and looks at Ray again.

"Yeah. 100%" he replies before asking Ray,

"So, what you gonna do about the football match on Sunday?"

"I don't know, man" replies Ray with a lost look on his face as they both walk down the high street.

CHAPTER THREE

SEMI INTENTIONS

2 DAYS LATER...

TUESDAY 19th APRIL 2016...

07:02 am, Joe and April's house...

With Denny and Izzy downstairs in the living room eating their breakfast and watching television, April tiptoes upstairs in her dressing gown towards the bedroom where Joe is sleeping. She creeps around the door to see Joe fast asleep on the morning of his birthday.

April unties her dressing gown and softly climbs onto Joe putting her head under the cover to wake him up with a surprise. As Joe is waking up, April moves up onto him and starts riding him in a quick birthday morning romp.

Over in just two minutes, Joe is still sleepy from being woken up. He rubs his face as April kisses him on the forehead and whispers in his ear.

"Happy birthday babe", she giggles and climbs off him, running off to the bathroom. She leaves Joe lying on his back looking at the ceiling. He sits up, rubbing his eyes now ready to get out of bed.

April returns from the toilet and pops her head around the bedroom door.

"Kids are waiting for you downstairs" she tells Joe, just getting up from bed to open the curtains slightly for some light.

April runs downstairs and into the living room where Denny and Izzy are watching television.

"Quick, quick! Daddy will be down in a sec" she quietly tells the kids who are both sitting glued to the tele channel. They get up and get the cards and presents they have made and bought for him.

Joe walks down the stairs and into the living room as April pulls a party popper covering Joe with coloured tinsel.

"HAPPY BIRTHDAY DADDY!" yell April, Denny and Izzy together. Izzy runs up to her Daddy to give him a big hug, and the birthday card she made. April kisses Joe and tells him,

"Now I am going for a shower" she smiles giddily at Joe.

Over at Ray and Kirsty's...

Kirsty is about to leave for work while Ray is still in bed having only just woken up. She walks into the bedroom with a cup of tea for Ray, putting it on the side.

"There you go. Right, I am off to work" Kirsty says as she walks back towards the bedroom door before turning around and asking Ray,

"Have you booked anywhere yet? It's this weekend you know."

Ray, still half-asleep, mutters back,

"Yeah, I am going to book it today babe" he says rubbing his eyes and grabbing his little wooden box containing his smoking tools. He opens the box and pulls a Rizla paper out.

Kirsty smiles at Ray about the booking of the restaurant for their anniversary but then rolls her eyes seeing Ray start to roll a spliff as soon as he has woken up. She leaves for work and, hearing the front door slam, Ray knows he needs to book a good restaurant, and sort the issue of the football match tickets, if he is not going to the match in just five days' time.

Meanwhile…

Troy is still pondering on what to do next about his fears of Joe going legal and quitting buying cocaine from him as the week goes on.

FRIDAY 22nd APRIL…

Joe is asleep in bed; April and the kids are awake and downstairs watching TV.

Joe's alarm goes off and Joe gets up, pulling the curtains open to stare out the window for a few moments. April brings a cup of tea for Joe who is deep in thought, looking out the window.

"Morning babe. You OK?" April asks Joe, seeing him in thought about something. She gives him his tea.

"Yeah, I'm all good gorgeous. Just a shit sleep" replies Joe.

April is not convinced.

"You sure?" April asks again.

"Yeah babe, I'll be fine" says Joe trying not to show the worry of what might happen when Joe tells Troy he is quitting.

April gives Joe a kiss on the forehead and leaves the bedroom to go back downstairs to continue watching TV with the kids.

Joe watches April leave the bedroom then picks up his phone. Continuing to be deeply in thought about what he is going to tell Troy, he hopes that after today, it will be the end of it.

Over at Troy's...

Troy is awake, standing in front of the mirror looking at himself in his dressing gown. There is a half-naked girl lying in his bed. He walks across the room to his desk, turns his laptop on and looks at Joe's business page. He scrolls through all the winning bets and positive comments on screen, he does not like what he sees. He has a very angry look on his face.

Back at Joe's house...

Joe is in the shower and April has just made breakfast for the kids.

Joe gets out of the shower and starts to get dressed when his phone rings, it's Ray calling.

"Good morning Raymondo" Joe says, answering the phone.

"Is it?" replies a depressed Ray, who is sitting in bed rolling himself a spliff.

Joe gets dressed, puts Ray on loudspeaker and places the phone on the side.

"Bundle of joy this morning ain't you?"

"You sorted your little problem out yet?" asks Joe.

"No, not yet" replies Ray.

"It's your funeral" Joe says, still getting dressed.

Ray changes the subject.

"So, what's your plan for today? And what we gonna do with these notes?" he asks Joe.

Joe is now dressed and looking out of his bedroom window.

"Today is the day I talk to Troy" Joe replies.

Ray lights up his spliff.

"What, about you leaving the alliance?" Ray enquires.

Joe is looking impressed,

"Big words for you this early!"

"Well, it's got to happen sometime, so fuck it."

"And I don't know yet, let me deal with Troy first, then we will take care of them notes. I'll bell you in a bit" informs Joe as he puts his shoes on.

Ray puts down the phone and finishes rolling his spliff when Kirsty comes storming into the room.

"Are you going to do anything constructive today?" Kirsty asks Ray with a serious look on her face.

Ray looks up at Kirsty and she fires into him again.

"Like sort out what we are doing this weekend… Not getting stoned or football."

Ray is feeling sorry for himself.

"Yeah babe, I've sorted it" Ray declares, knowing he hasn't yet but bluffs Kirsty to save more grief.

Kirsty looks at Ray suspiciously, unsure what to think.

"I'm going to work. See you later" Kirsty tells Ray before shutting the bedroom door and leaving the house.

The front door shuts, and Ray lies back down looking at the ceiling with a worried look on his face. He is aware that he has falsely informed his girlfriend that he has sorted out what and where they are going for their 5-year anniversary which is in just over 24 hours' time.

Meanwhile back at Joe's…

April has dealt with the kids and is now making herself and Joe a cooked breakfast, bacon, eggs, beans, and toast are all on the go.

Joe comes down from upstairs after having a shower and getting dressed, he sits down at the kitchen table. April puts two cups of tea down on the table, one for each of them.

"What's your POA today?" April asks Joe.

"Well," Joe says, while taking a sip of his tea.

"I gotta go see that John at some point after speaking with Troy."

April puts Joe's plate of food on the table.

"You still going with the plan then?"

"John? What Big John?" April asks.

Joe is tired of explaining why Big John is known as Little John.

"Yeah, no… Little John, but yeah, anyway" says Joe to April who looks slightly confused.

"It will be the last time I'm picking up anything like that up" he says as April puts the salt and pepper on the table in front of him.

"You sure you want to do this?" April says as she puts her plate of breakfast down on the table and sits down before Joe says,

"Babe, I've been ducking and diving my whole life."

"I need to think about you and the kids. It's time."

April smiles and holds Joe's arm,

"I totally agree babe".

Back at Ray's...

Ray is standing on the balcony smoking his spliff, his phone in his hand. He is looking for date night ideas, time running out for him to book somewhere for the anniversary meal.

Ray puts his phone to his ear to make a call,

"Hello… you got a table free for tomorrow night?"

Meanwhile…

Joe and April finish their breakfast and Joe goes upstairs to grab his phone and sit on the bed pondering what he is going to say to Troy.

Joe makes the call.

At Troy's…

Troy is sitting at his table eating toast with fruit when Joe calls his phone.

He picks up his phone, answering it.

"Good morning Joe, bit early ain't it?" Troy says, looking at his watch.

Joe is sitting on his bed,

"Yeah, morning Troy. There is something I need to talk with you about."

Troy stops eating and sits up, ready for what Joe is about to say.

"What's that then?" Troy asks Joe.

Joe continues to tell Troy,

"I will be seeing John later. But it will be the last time I do."

"I'm out. I got another thing on, and I just need to stop doing this, I got my family to think about."

"I'm done."

Troy knew Joe was doing other things but didn't expect Joe to end their business together so soon.

"Really? Well, that is a shame Joe, we work well together" says Troy casually, hiding his anger.

"Troy, I don't want any trouble. I just want out" Joe says.

Troy looks out of his window.

"Well, I can't say I ain't disappointed Joe. As I said, I think we worked well."

"OK, I guess I will see you around then" Troy says before putting the phone down on Joe, looking quite unhappy about the news.

Troy then picks back up his phone to ring Little John.

"John, you were right. Joe's just rang me to tell me your meet with him later will be the last."

Little John is sitting in his car on the phone to Troy,

"Well, we'll see about that. I'll take care of it, Boss."

SUNDAY, 24th APRIL 2016...

Today is the day...

The day that will define Joe's future... and maybe Ray and Kirsty's relationship.

Joe has just told Troy of his plan, to leave the game and crack on with his, so far successful, online business, and Troy has, apparently, given Joe his blessing. However, that is not actually the case and Little John is hatching a plan to keep Joe working with them.

Ray doesn't have it much better, depending on how you look at it, having to choose between disappointing Kirsty or the most dangerous person on the planet is a hard call.

He must deal with the dilemma of his beloved Crystal Palace FC playing at Wembley in a massive game, which he purchased tickets for, being on the same day as his five-year anniversary with Kirsty. She has no interest in football and will be expecting a nice restaurant or a trip to the theatre.

As well as this, Ray and Joe have invested in £70,000 worth of fake bank notes and these also need to be dealt with. Joe isn't too happy with the whole thing. He now needs to offload them, get his investment back and do what he set out to do, which is not all this shit. So now it's time to start to think about how they are going to get rid of the paper.

7:06am...

Ray has just sneaked out of bed and tiptoed out of the bedroom before Kirsty wakes up. He quickly writes in an anniversary card, popping it in the envelope and leaving it on the kitchen side before sneaking out of the house very quietly and heading to the cafe.

Outside the newspaper shop displays posters exclaiming,

"FA CUP SEMI FINALS... CRYSTAL PALACE V WATFORD"

This part of south London is alight, buzzing for the big day. A win today and Crystal Palace FC would reach their first FA cup final since 1990.

In the café...

Ray walks through the café door and is welcomed as soon as he enters.

"Aye Aye Ray. Big day today" says Bleu the café lady from behind the counter as Ray comes through the door and up to the counter.

"Usual? Set 3, extra egg and sausage?" Bleu asks Ray.

"Nah, just a tea please Bleu. Might have something to eat in a bit" replies Ray looking fed up.

"You OK Ray? Not like you before a big football day."

"Gonna be a long day up to Wembley and back" Bleu says looking slightly concerned.

Ray looks even more glum at this point, walks over to a table, and takes a seat. Bleu brings Ray's tea and puts it on the table as Ray pulls the tickets for the football from his jacket pocket.

Kirsty has just woken up in bed noticing Ray is not there. She gets up, putting her dressing gown on, she leaves the bedroom calling Ray as she walks down the hallway.

Ray is sitting at the café table with his match tickets for today's game looking lost when Bleu brings a cup of tea to another customer sitting near Ray's table. She places it on the table and looks across at Ray, unsure what is wrong, just as a man and his son walk into the café.

"Morning!" Bleu says to the man as he takes a seat with his son, who is about 9 years old and wearing a Crystal Palace football shirt and scarf wrapped around him.

"We going to win today?" Bleu asks the boy, who cheekily nods back.

At Ray's, Kirsty walks into the kitchen and sees her card. She opens it giving it a quick read and then puts it back on the kitchen side with no real emotion. She is still wondering what Ray has planned and assumes he has gone to the football as he is up and out early. She walks back into the bedroom, angrily slamming the door.

Back in the café...

Ray is still totally gutted he must choose between going to the game and taking Kirsty out.

The man, a couple of tables over with his son, is on the phone to the mother of the young boy.

"I don't know yet, we are going to go to the park and then try to watch the game somewhere" the man reports.

There is a couple of seconds pause and the man then says,

"Michelle… I can't afford to do much else!"

There is an audible rant from the other side before the phone goes dead.

The man looks over to Ray as he has just witnessed the phone call, as he is only a couple of tables from them.

"Women aye?" the man says to Ray.

"Tell me about it!" Ray replies, looking at the young boy in his Crystal Palace shirt and then looking back at his tickets in his hand.

Meanwhile...

Joe is up, making himself a cup of tea as he rings Ray, also eager to know if Ray has got himself out of the pickle he is in.

Ray is still sitting in the café when his phone starts to ring.

"Easy bro" Ray answers the phone with a slightly dull tone.

Joe is at home on the phone, now back lying in bed with April.

"Raymondo! So, what are you doing today?"

"Oh, and happy anniversary!"

"Yeah, I have booked a table for tonight."

"I don't know what I'm going to do with these tickets" says Ray.

Joe gets up, leaving April in bed, and turns on his laptop.

"Sell them, someone will want them" Joe says.

Ray looks across at the man and his son at the next table. He is conscious that the young boy is a Palace supporter and not going to the game today as he heard the poor Dad getting grief from the boy's Mum.

"Yeah, I'll sort it" Ray replies.

At home, Kirsty is getting in the shower still awaiting news of where they are going.

Troy is awake, lying in bed with his two half-naked girlfriends, staring at the ceiling deep in thought.

Little John is also up, already on today's task. He opens a drawer in his living room and picks out a camera before leaving the house and getting into his car.

April is now up and getting Denny ready for their local Sunday morning kid's football match. Joe is on his laptop, holding Izzy in his arms.

Back at the café...

Ray finishes his third cup of tea, gets up from the table and walks towards the door. He passes the man with his son.

"Hello mate" Ray says to the man, then turns to the young boy.

"We gonna win today?"

The boy smiles and says, "Yeah. 2-1!"

Ray then turns back to the man,

"Would you be able to get to Wembley today?"

The man looks confused. "What?" he says to Ray, totally baffled by the question.

"To the game" Ray replies.

"I ain't got tickets mate" he says, smiling at Ray, still unsure of what Ray is pursuing.

Ray drops the tickets on the table in front of the man, the young boy looks down at the tickets with amazement.

"Have a great day" Ray says, winking at the man and smiling at the boy. He then pays for his three cups of tea plus the bill for the dad with his son and then walks out of the café.

The father in total shock watches Ray leave and smiles, looking at his son.

"Are we going to Wembley, Dad?" the boy asks his father.

"Looks like we are son!" he says still smiling, the young boy now overjoyed.

Leaving the café and walking down the high street Ray makes a call on his phone.

"Yeah hello, can I order a big bunch of flowers, please?"

09:51 am...

April and Denny leave for Denny's football match, whilst Joe and their daughter Izzy stay at home for the morning.

Just down the road, in sight of Joe's house, Little John is sitting in his car waiting for April to come out with at least one of her children. As she leaves with Denny, both getting in the car and driving off, Little John takes some photographs with the camera he brought with him. Waiting a couple of seconds before starting the car engine he begins to follow April's car.

Ray collects the bunch of flowers from the local florist and heads home, where Kirsty has been slowly getting herself ready for the day, putting on make-up and doing her hair before getting dressed.

April arrives at the local kid's Sunday morning football match. Loads of kids are gathered in their football kits with parents all around the side-lines. Little John pulls up, again down the road, but in sight of the match. He grabs his phone and puts it to his ear, watching April and Denny.

Joe is at home with Izzy who is watching TV, Joe walks into the room with Izzy's jacket.

"Come and put your coat on, we are going to the park" Joe says to his daughter just as his phone rings.

LITTLE JOHN CALLING… Joe sees on his phone screen. Joe answers the phone.

"John" Joe says into the phone.

Little John is sitting in his car watching Joe's missus and son.

"Joe, Troy needs you to do him a favour, for you leaving all of a sudden."

Joe looks slightly worried but he always knew it was too good to be true to get away from the likes of Troy and Little John that easily, he replies,

"And what's that then?"

"Meet me at the entrance of the underground car park… Tonight, 8PM." Little John tells Joe before putting the phone down and picking up his camera, getting ready to take more photos.

Joe puts his phone back in his pocket and puts the coat on his daughter and they leave. Joe is looking pissed off now.

A little later...

Ray comes home after being out for nearly four hours, bringing back the bunch of flowers and a box of chocolates. He surprises Kirsty as he walks in the bedroom. Kirsty is brushing her hair and smiles at Ray.

"What time are we going out?" asks Kirsty looking at Ray, hoping for an answer.

"Be ready for half 6" Ray replies as he walks up to Kirsty putting the chocolates on the bed and giving her the flowers. He kisses her on the forehead and says,

"I'm going to try catch some of the football", before walking out of the bedroom.

Kirsty's face goes from sweet to sour again as she realises there is still a couple of hours until they go out and Ray will be stuck to the television screen watching what he can before it's time to leave the house.

6:09 pm, Troy's house...

Little John has come back from his day's duties with printed photographs in an envelope of Joe's missus and young son. He explains his plan to Troy,

"Right Boss, everything is in place. Joe will take the goods to look after."

"Then the boys on the estate will do their job" John tells Troy.

"OK… You sure you can trust these Lads?" Troy asks.

"They won't let us down Boss" John replies.

"So, what's the photos for, John?" Troy asks.

"Just in case our friend needs reminding what's at stake" says John looking at Troy with confidence.

Troy smiles with joy at the plan.

"Good work John" he nods his head, content.

6:40pm, Ray and Kirsty's house…

Kirsty is ready to go when Ray said to be. Ray has only been able to watch the football match on television when he was supposed to be at the stadium. Crystal Palace win 2-1 and make it their first cup final since 1990. This puts Ray in a great mood but also means he has left it late to get ready to go out once the match finished, which Kirsty is none too pleased about.

Joe and April's house...

Joe is in the kitchen and, as usual, on his laptop checking the day's football and betting results when April walks in with a holiday brochure. She puts it down in front of Joe and wraps her arms around him.

Joe picks up the brochure.

"I get the hint" he says, smiling at April then looking back to his laptop.

April standing over Joe, says,

"Well, I thought it would be nice to get away."

"Like a celebration, your new business, getting out, going legal and all that."

She leans in and gives Joe another cuddle.

"Yeah, go on then. It's a good idea."

"Just let me know when you are booking it for" says Joe.

April smiles, gives Joe a big kiss on his cheek and happily leaves him to his work.

Joe looks up at the kitchen clock, knowing he has to meet Little John in about 20 minutes' time.

Meanwhile on anniversary date night...

Ray and Kirsty are sitting at a table in the restaurant Ray had booked earlier, a local Italian on the high street. Ray is happy, Crystal Palace are in the FA cup final, and he has a plate of food in front of him that he is tucking into.

"This is banging" says Ray with a mouthful of food, his head down in his plate.

Kirsty is not impressed at all, Ray left it too late, and her favourite restaurant was fully booked.

She swirls her food around her plate with a look of disgust on her face.

Underground car park, Brixton...

Joe is walking through the local estate on route to the underground car park to meet Little John.

Little John pulls up in his car as Joe turns the corner to the car park. John gets out of the car.

"Good evening, Joe" John greets Joe in a sarcastic tone.

Joe casually walks up to John.

"What the fuck is this all about John?" Joe asks.

"Well, since you up and left with very little notice, and you are the only one Troy trusts,"

"He needs you to look after the next couple of little parcels you would have had."

"Only be a week, just until we can replace you" John says starkly to Joe.

"Why me?" Joe asks, looking uncomfortable with the situation he is being put in.

John replies, "As I said, it was going to be yours… And Troy only trusts you".

Joe looks at John and says,

"Oh, thanks" sarcastically, shaking his head, before asking John, "Well, when am I taking it? I'm going on holiday soon."

Little John looks at Joe and walks towards the back of his car.

Back in the restaurant…

Ray is now tucking into his dessert, still looking happy with himself.

Kirsty pours another glass of wine for herself. She finishes the bottle but it does not fill her glass, so she waves over to the waiter for another bottle. She looks at Ray still eating, she is not impressed but Kirsty is still going to enjoy her night by drinking as much as she can.

Outside the underground car park, Little John opens the boot of his car. Joe is now standing next to him to see what is in the boot.

"Fucking hell John. A couple of little parcels? There's six months' worth there" Joe says dramatically, nodding at the parcel and looking at John.

John turns to Joe,

"See you in about a week." He passes the parcel towards Joe.

Just down the road in view of Joe and Little John, waiting for Joe to leave with the parcel, are the Lads Jay, Neil, Si and William from the estate. They have been told to follow Joe after he leaves John to see where Joe takes the valuable parcel containing around £60,000 worth of cocaine. William, however, does not really want to be involved.

All four Lads are sitting in the car watching Joe from a distance. Will, sitting in the back ready to get out of the car, says to the other Lads, "Boys, I ain't really on this. I might duck out." Jayson grabs Will before he can leave.

"What ya doing man? We are going to get seen. Just fucking stay here ya pussy." He tells Will who is sulking on the back seat not wanting anything to do with it.

9:37pm, cocktail bar, Brixton...

Ray and Kirsty have finished their dinner date and moved on to a cocktail bar. Kirsty is sitting at the bar on her own as Ray goes to the toilet when a random guy in the bar approaches Kirsty and tries to make a move on her by asking if she wants a drink.

"What you drinking?" says the guy to Kirsty smiling at her.

Kirsty looks at the guy with a stern face and replies, "No thank you, I'm here with someone."

The guy is still keen.

"That's cool, maybe take my number then?" he asks, clearly not getting the message.

Kirsty goes to take a sip of her drink but on hearing what the guy is up to suddenly pauses her drink and puts it back down. She looks at the guy with an even sterner look on her face and calmly replies,

"Do yourself a favour before I rip your bollocks off and shove 'em down your throat."

The guy's face slowly drops as he realises Kirsty isn't to be played with like that, and slowly walks away into the crowd.

Kirsty picks her drink back up, takes a sip and then looks around to see if Ray has come out of the toilet. She spots Ray on the dance floor with a group of lads all celebrating the win Crystal Palace had only hours ago.

Kirsty rolls her eyes and calls the bartender for another drink, whilst Ray dances and hugs the fellow football fans.

After meeting John and taking the parcel to look after, Joe walks about seven minutes across the estate. The Lads, on orders from Little John, are now following Joe on foot without Joe seeing them. Joe reaches his lock up, unlocks the door and walks in, shutting the door behind him.

The Lads watch and wait, hidden behind a car about 100 yards away.

Inside the lock up...

Joe puts the parcel in a drawer, then puts paperwork over to cover it before shutting that drawer and opening the drawer above.

In the open drawer are the fake banknotes. Joe picks them up and starts putting them in his inside coat pocket and jean pockets until he has every last banknote neatly filling every one of his pockets. He leaves the lock up, shutting the door and sets off for home. All the while being watched by The Lads who notice that the parcel Joe entered with, he has left without.

Now knowing where Joe's safekeeping place is for Troy's parcel, when Joe is out of sight, The Lads walk up to the lock up to check out how they will get in and steal the parcel, as ordered by Little John.

CHAPTER FOUR

BLUE

MONDAY

MONDAY, 25th APRIL

8:31am…

The Monday morning after the night before…

Ray is up and making himself a fried egg sandwich in the kitchen, listening to the radio talk about yesterday's big win for Crystal Palace and starts singing to himself,

"We're going to Wembley" while having a dance, frying some bacon.

In the bedroom, hungover Kirsty is still in bed, smudged make-up still on from last night. She hears Ray singing in the next room and pushes the duvet cover off her. She is still half-dressed wearing last night's clothes, looking rather worse for wear.

Kirsty, eyes hardly open, throws her arm to the bedside unit to grab her phone but drops the phone on the floor.

Moaning, she throws a little fit before sitting up to pick her phone up from the floor.

In the Davies household it's a normal Monday morning, with April getting Denny and Izzy ready for school and Joe working on his online business in the kitchen.

Joe still has the hump about having to look after Troy's parcel and has not told April yet.

Izzy comes into the kitchen to give Joe a hug while April puts Denny's coat on in the hallway.

April yells, "IZZY... COME AND PUT YOUR COAT ON PLEASE." April walks into the kitchen with Izzy's coat in her hand, she sees her clinging on to her dad. April smiles and walks over to them.

"How's business?" April asks, looking at the laptop and then telling Izzy to put her coat on.

Joe replies, "Yeah not bad, still early days but doing better than I thought I would at this stage. So, all good so far."

April kisses Joe, "I'll be back in about 45 minutes."

She smiles at Joe as she takes Izzy off him. Izzy waves at Joe and he smiles back, blowing her a kiss as April carries her away. April leaves the house, puts both the kids in the car and drives them to school.

As April leaves, Joe pulls the drawer next to him open and pulls out a sealed plastic bag with the neatly packed wad of bank notes in it. He looks at them deep in thought about what he is going to do with them. He takes them upstairs to put them on top of the wardrobe, out of reach of anyone in the house.

Meanwhile…

Half a mile away at Joe's lock up, a break-in has clearly taken place. The door is vandalised and open slightly.

Joe is still at home and, as yet, none the wiser.

EIGHT HOURS PREVIOUSLY

1:08am…

After the Lads spied on Joe leaving his lock up without the parcel he entered with, they all decided to come back a few hours later in the early hours of the morning. They brought tools with them to break in quickly and quietly, getting through the door and entering the lock up.

Three of the four Lads searched around as William watched through the slightly open door they just broke in through, for anyone or police.

In the search, Jayson finds a pocket watch on the side and picks it up, putting it in his inside pocket. He looks around to see if any of the other Lads had seen him pick it up. They didn't, two were busy opening drawers and cupboards and the other was looking out.

It wasn't long before the parcel was found by one of the Lads, along with Joe's last bit in another drawer which was a bonus for the Lads. They only had orders to retrieve the parcel John gave Joe that night, anything else was the Lads' to keep.

So, in all, a bit of cash in a drawer and a nice little package of coke for themselves in another. As well as successfully getting Troy's parcel which they will collect a payment for on its return to Little John.

1:50am...

Little John is falling asleep on his sofa at home when his phone rings, waking him up.

John answers it.

"Yeah?" he says, in a tired voice.

On hearing the Lads have done what was asked, John wakes up a bit more.

"Already? You sure you got the parcel?"

The Lad, Simon, tells John that he has the parcel, and he is five minutes away. He wants to meet John to exchange the parcel for the payment promised, ASAP.

John sits up and looks at the watch on his wrist.

"Fucking hell, you don't hang about. OK, see you in ten minutes" John replies before putting the phone down, yawning and sleepily getting up to go and meet the Lads at this late hour.

Joe is at home in bed asleep with April after coming home from meeting John, dropping the parcel to the lock up for safekeeping and then getting down for the night.

2:06am...

Ray and Kirsty are drinking a row of shots from the bar in the cocktail bar they have been in for a few hours.

Both clearly drunk and enjoying the night together, dancing drunkenly at the bar now with only a few other party goers.

On the estate…

Little John pulls up to the normal meeting place with the Lads, an archway near the housing estate. The Lads are already waiting for John.

"Well, that was quick" John says as he gets out of his car and walks towards them.

"You get the right parcel?" John asks Neil who is standing there with a bag.

The Lad hands the bag to John and John opens it to look inside at the contents.

"Nice work Lads" John nodding his head, impressed with the Lads' work.

John pulls an envelope packed with £2000 in cash and gives it to the Lad in return for the parcel. He then addresses all four Lads,

"The most important thing is that nobody can know this happened. Got it?" looking around at all four standing in front of him.

Back to the morning after...

9:25am...

Ray is on his balcony smoking a spliff after eating his sandwiches. Kirsty is still in bed hungover, after having to call in sick to work again. This time claiming she has food poisoning rather than telling work she really just drank far too much last night, sinking two bottles of wine in the restaurant, then cocktails and shots until nearly 3am.

At Joe's...

April comes home from doing the school run. Joe is upstairs getting dressed into some jogging bottoms and a hoodie as he is going for a run.

April sees Joe is not in the kitchen and goes upstairs and into the bedroom where Joe has just got changed into his running gear.

"I've booked the holiday for the last week of July." April says to Joe walking up to him.

"You said to let you know dates." April says while stroking his arm lightly.

"Yeah, sweet babe, I'll note it down" Joe replies.

"Where are you off to?" April asks Joe, stroking him more.

"Park... some stretches and a few laps" Joe replies looking down, smiling at April as she walks to bed before climbing onto it looking at Joe and says,

"Why don't you do stretches and laps... here... with me?" looking at Joe in a way no man could resist his wife.

Joe thinks for a second in a dilemma, but he looks at April lying there looking seductively at him.

Joe closes the door and takes his shirt off as he walks towards April lying on the bed waiting for him.

Little John is up and about and on his way to Troy's to let him know the good news and deliver the parcel Troy wanted back. Upon knocking the front door, he is once again, greeted by one of Troy's half-naked girlfriends.

At Ray and Kirsty's...

Ray brings Kirsty a cup of coffee in bed to help her feel a bit more normal before she finally gets out of bed. She is clearly still affected by the amount of alcohol she consumed only hours ago, even though Ray feels fine.

"I shouldn't of drank that wine... both bottles!"

Kirsty says to Ray as he puts her coffee down and leaves again knowing he got away with the whole anniversary thing by the skin of his teeth.

Back at Joe and April's house...

In the bedroom, Joe and April lie in bed after having sex, both now in a t-shirt and boxer shorts. April's legs are over Joe's, and she is smiling with her eyes closed, looking tired, hugging him.

"So, did your plan go... as planned, with Big John, or Little John whatever?" April asks Joe.

"Yeah, sort of. It will be all over next week for sure" Joe replies stroking April's head as they both lie on the bed, still unaware of the break-in of his lock up.

Meanwhile at Troy's...

Little John has arrived carrying a bag with the parcel in it that Troy had given him, to give to Joe to then get the Lads to steal.

Little John places the bag on the table in front of Troy just as he is about to eat a bowl of cereal. Troy looks in the bag and then picks it up and places it behind him.

"Better put that over there" he says, putting the bag down and then turning back around to John.

"Don't want any of that over my cornflakes" winking at John and sitting back down to his bowl of cereal.

"So, that's £60k our friend Joe owes us, one way or another" Troy says to John while eating his cereal. John responds,

"I will give it a couple more days, then I will ask to collect the parcel. Obviously he won't have it, so we will work with him to pay it off slowly. Meaning… he will have to stay on working for us" he tells Troy.

Troy agrees and replies,

"Or… it's a £60 grand debt out of his own pocket."

John is not looking confident.

"I doubt very much he has got that. But I suppose you never know" he replies.

Troy pulls out a big envelope from his drawer and hands it to John and says,

"Good work John."

Meanwhile…

Ray decides to leave the house to go for a walk and another little smoke. He tries to ring Joe, but Joe's phone is downstairs in the kitchen and Joe is still upstairs in bed with April. Ray doesn't get an answer so heads to the café for a takeaway cup of tea to go with his spliff.

On route to the café, Ray must pass Joe's lock up.

He walks past and sees the door slightly damaged and open. Ray walks up to the lock up confused at what he is seeing and gets out his phone to try and get hold of Joe again.

By now, April is in the shower, so Joe walks downstairs to have a cigarette and get his phone. Grabbing his phone, he sees a few missed calls from Ray.

Joe steps out to his back garden, lights a cigarette up and rings Ray back.

Ray is in the lock up now looking around at the mess left by the burglary, he answers his phone to Joe who is calling him back.

"Bro, please tell me you took the notes out of the lock up" Ray asks, looking around the lock up.

"I took them last night funny enough. I got them here at home, why?" Joe replies.

"Thank fuck for that" Ray says.

"Bro, I'm in the lock up. You've had a break-in."

Joe pauses with shock, "What??"

"What do you mean you're in the lock up?" demands Joe.

Ray looks around at the mess.

"Yeah bro, get yourself around here. I'll wait for ya" replies Ray before putting down the phone.

Joe, looking very worried, stubs his cigarette out and quickly goes back inside and upstairs to get dressed. He must go now to go and inspect the lock up after what Ray has just told him.

Joe is about to leave the bedroom after throwing on some clothes as April gets out of the shower with a towel around her. She sees Joe quickly going down the stairs.

"YOU STILL GOING FOR THAT RUN YEAH BABE?" April, smiling, yells down the stairs at Joe.

Joe flies out of the house without answering her, leaving April looking a little confused at the top of the stairs, just as her phone starts to ring.

At Ray and Kirsty's...

Kirsty, also just out of the shower, towel around her and feeling a little bit better now picks up her phone to call April, sitting down on her sofa.

"Alright, babe?" says Kirsty, her head back on the sofa turning off the TV that Ray left on before going out.

"Ahh, I called in work sick earlier" she informs April.

"Good night then?" April asks, getting dressed having just had a shower.

A hungover Kirsty, looking tired and a bit disappointed, replies,

"Not really, the restaurant was shit, and Ray was on the dance floor singing football songs with strangers until the early hours. Then we got chucked out of a taxi for being sick… in the taxi."

"Oh really? Take it Ray drunk a lot then" April asks as she puts on her bra.

Kirsty replies,

"No, I was the one sick in the taxi, I drank far too much. It was a good idea at the time" she says, switching the television back on.

"Yeah, it always is the night before" says April, smiling, now almost fully dressed.

Kirsty is still sloughed on the sofa,

"I might pop up this afternoon if you're home?" she asks April.

April is tying her hair up.

"Yeah, come and do the school run with me, then you can tell me all about last night" she replies.

Both April and Kirsty are starting to get ready for the day as Joe approaches his lock up door. He sees it is damaged and open. He walks in to see Ray standing there shaking his head.

Joe walks straight over to the drawer he put Troy's parcel in. The drawer now only has a few sheets of paperwork in, the parcel gone.

He puts his head in his hands.

"Fuck, shit, bollocks" he yells, panic setting in.

"What's up? What's missing bro?" asks Ray.

Joe turns to him and says,

"Troy's parcel I was looking after."

Looking confused, Ray asks,

"I thought you were done with that".

Joe checks the other drawers where he had some cash and his last bit of work from Troy,

"And my bit of work, plus my petty cash"

"Great, I'm about three grand down, and now I'm in Troy's pocket" says Joe, looking at Ray with a worried look on his face.

Ray, still confused about the whole situation, asks Joe,

"So, what the fuck has actually happened here?"

Joe explains, "That meeting with John last night, well I got pushed into holding what he had for me before I gave my notice."

"I bought it back here last night. That's when I took the fake notes home."

"I didn't want everything here, and I ain't taking drugs home so..."

Ray, still looking confused, asks Joe,

"So, this parcel you're looking after, that is now missing, how big is this parcel?"

"At least £50k, probably more knowing Troy" Joe says, shaking his head, wondering what the fuck he is going to do now.

Ray asks, "When does Troy want it back?"

"Any time in the next week" Joe replies, now with his hands over his face.

Ray asks Joe,

"So, what are you gonna tell Troy then?"

Joe removes his hands from covering his face, looks at Ray and says,

"I don't know yet Ray, stop with all the fucking questions will ya... I can't think".

Ray puffs out his cheeks and lights up the spliff he was saving to go with a tea from the café. He takes a puff of it when Joe takes it out of his hand and starts puffing on it.

"Bro, what are you doing? You don't smoke weed" Ray says to Joe, looking confused as Joe puffs away on the spliff then passes it back to Ray.

Joe looks around the lock up and notices his pocket watch is gone from the shelf it was on. The pocket watch that Joe inherited from his grandad and has a lot of sentimental value. This leaves Joe feeling even more angry.

2:11pm, London City Airport…

Ray's uncle Rupert, former ruler of these parts of south London, has just landed back in the UK from a three-week holiday in Mexico with his wife Rose.

Rupert and Rose exit the airport with Rupert looking around, breathing in the air, happy to back home in England, Rose not so much.

"Ain't it cold?" Rose, shivering, says to Rupert who is just in a t-shirt but not bothered at all. He looks for his driver to take them home to Brixton.

Over at Ray and Kirsty's…

Kirsty has just left home and is on her way to April's for a catch up on last night's anniversary date night antics, as well as to go and pick up the kids with April.

Joe has called someone out to fix the lock up door and now both Joe and Ray are sitting in the café. Ray is drinking a tea, Joe, a bottle of water.

Joe is looking a bit stressed as his phone starts to ring, thinking it will be April.

"That will be April wondering where I've got to" Joe says as he takes the phone out of his pocket and looks at the screen.

"Oh, it's your uncle" Joe says to Ray before answering.

"Hello mate" Joe answers the phone, then listens to what Rupert says to him.

"OK mate, I'll pop round soon" Joe says before putting the phone down.

Ray looking at Joe intrigued, asks, "What's up?"

Joe replies "He has just got back off holiday, he wants some smoke."

"He's asked me to get some from you and drop it up to him. Why don't he phone you Ray?" Joe asks, confused why Rupert doesn't just get his own nephew to drop it to him.

Ray takes a sip of his cup of tea and says, "I don't know, he just don't like me in his house. Says I'm clumsy and stupid".

Joe looks at Ray,

"Well sort that out for me please as got enough on my plate right now".

Ray picks out a small bag of weed and passes it across the table to Joe in full view of everyone in the café.

Joe grabs it quickly looking around the café then quietly says to Ray,

"I see what your uncle means" looking at Ray, shaking his head with disbelief, Ray looks confused, as normal.

3:10pm, Crawford Primary School, Camberwell...

The school bell is heard from outside the school gates as parents pile in and wait in the playground for their children. The school entrance door opens and dozens of kids come flocking out into the playground.

April and Kirsty are also standing in the playground waiting for Denny and Izzy, talking about last night.

"April, we don't even get a takeaway from the place because it is horrible".

Kirsty is talking to April about the restaurant Ray booked for their anniversary, just as Denny and Izzy come walking out of the school building looking around the playground for their Mum.

April waves to the kids then replies to Kirsty,

"At least he didn't go to the football babe, I know he wanted to go to that... a lot of people wanted to."

Both kids run up to April and Kirsty and all four head for the exit of the playground to start to walk home.

"Auntie Kirsty is coming for dinner."

April says to the kids as they leave the school playground.

On the estate...

The Lads who just broke into Joe's lock up, only 12 hours ago, are still awake. They are all drinking and sniffing Joe's bit of coke, sharing out cash from the lock up and the payment from Little John. They have music on in one of the Lads' bedrooms at home. Still in party mode, celebrating after their little earner last night, as well as knowing Little John and Troy were happy with the result. Jayson who has not had as much drink and drugs as the other Lads decides to leave the bedroom telling the other three Lads,

"I'll be back soon".

One of the other Lads, Neil asks,

"Where are you going?" and then demands,

"Bring back more beers" as Jay leaves the bedroom.

After leaving the bedroom and the flat where all four Lads have been partying since leaving Little John, Jayson walks towards the high street. He puts his hand in his pocket and pulls out the pocket watch he slipped in there without the other Lads seeing. Jay's plan is to take the pocket watch to the pawn shop and chop it in for some extra cash.

A little later…

Joe turns up at Rupert's house, he and his wife Rose have only been back in the country a few hours. Rose brings drinks in for Rupert and Joe who are sitting on the sofa in the living room.

"So, how's that nephew of mine?" Rupert says to Joe sitting across from him.

Joe smiles and pulls out the bag of weed Ray gave Joe in the café. He hands it to Rupert before replying, "Ray's good, still trying to keep him outta trouble" he says, with a little smile to Rupert.

Rupert takes the small bag of weed and smells it before saying, "Ain't had a smoke in nearly a month bruv. Yeah, lucky he's got you, the silly boy" he says to Joe.

Rupert then looks at what Joe is wearing and asks,

"You going running or something?"

Joe half laughs and asks how the holiday was, did he enjoy himself, did Rose enjoy herself? Rupert responds,

"Yeah, it was good man, but I'm glad to be back, ya know?"

"Anyway, what's happening with you?"

"How's business? I hear that Troy has got most of the land."

Joe explains all of what has happened in the last month, including Joe giving Troy notice of him leaving that work and life behind him. Rupert is instantly suspicious when Joe tells him that Troy wanted Joe to look after a parcel. Even more so now that Joe's lock up has been broken into and Troy's parcel is missing.

A shocked Rupert exclaims,

"What on earth has gone on?"

"Joe, I thought you were the smart one. Why did you even take anything off Troy when you told him basically you won't be on his books anymore and won't be making him money... think about it Joe" Rupert says shaking his head.

"Yeah, I know, it seemed like the easiest thing to do at time." Joe replies, deep in thought.

"I still don't know how anyone knew I took it back to the lock up" he says, looking confused.

Rupert leans over closer to Joe,

"Joe, don't underestimate Troy. He probably had you followed."

"Is there anyone else who knows you keep anything at that lock up and knows where the lock up is or been there before?" he asks Joe.

Joe pauses in thought then says,

"Yeah, there is someone."

Joe then adds that a pocket watch was taken in the raid and how it was his Grandad's, passed down to him when Joe's Grandad died.

Rupert thinks about how he can help,

"I will have a ring around and see if I can find anything out about all this." Rupert tells Joe.

The Lad with the pocket watch has left a local pawn shop after getting £350 for it. He heads back to join the other Lads after grabbing some beers.

Joe has left Rupert's and is just getting home after quite a mad day.

Joe walks through the door and straight through into the kitchen where April, Kirsty and kids are at the table eating their dinner. Joe is standing there in the clothes he put on for a run hours ago when April looks at him and says,

"Bloody hell babe, that was some run!"

Kirsty giggles, eating her dinner with the kids and April.

Joe braves it, smiles and heads upstairs to have a shower.

April sitting at the table sees something is up and gets up to follow Joe. April is at the bottom of the stairs and Joe is more than halfway up.

"Babe, are you okay?" April says to Joe.

Joe turns around to look at April at the bottom of the stairs. He smiles, "Yeah I'm cool".

He then continues upstairs for a much-needed shower. April watches him thoughtfully, knowing something is up before re-joining Kirsty and the kids in the kitchen.

Joe finally gets in the shower after one of the worst days of his life in some ways, and he is now even worse off than before he wanted to get out of all of this.

CHAPTER FIVE

POCKET

TUESDAY, 26TH APRIL…

8:17AM…

Joe is up and downstairs sitting in the kitchen at the laptop. He is struggling to focus on what he needs to do on his daily online business knowing Little John will be ringing him anytime in the next couple of days.

Joe picks up his phone and messages Ray to ring him. April and the kids come downstairs after getting ready for school. Both kids go into the living room and turn on the television. April walks through to the kitchen to make the kids breakfast.

"Hey babe" April says to Joe as she walks up to him and hugs him as he sits looking at the laptop.

"You alright? you didn't sleep well, you were tossing and turning all night".

 She says to Joe, looking concerned.

"Just another bad night's sleep, my back is playing up" Joe replies.

April rubs Joe's back,

"Getting old, babe" she says as she starts to make the kids' breakfast.

Joe is still not telling April what has happened at the lock up or about Troy's missing parcel. Obviously not wanting to worry her. More importantly, Joe doesn't know what he is going to do yet himself.

April takes the kids' breakfast into the living room as Joe's phone rings, RAY CALLING

Joe answers his phone.

"Morning bro, what's up?" asks Ray who is in bed, Kirsty has just left for work.

Joe talks softly so April can't hear much of the conversation,

"I need to see your mate billy" he says to Ray.

Ray looks confused.

"Billy? What do you want with Billy?" Ray asks Joe as he starts rolling a spliff.

"Because he is one of the only people to know where my lock up is and that anything is kept there. Probably wanted his fake notes back the thieving cunt." Joe says just before April comes back into the kitchen.

"Just get hold of him for me Ray" Joe says before putting the phone down.

April, looking concerned, asks Joe,

"Joe, what is going on? Something is up, I can tell. I know you".

Joe turns around to April and tells her,

"The lock up got broken into last night. Few things are missing, just trying to get them back. I'll sort it."

"Oh, shit really? OK, well why not just tell me?" April asks, looking confused at Joe.

"Because I am sorting it, so I don't have to tell you babe" Joe replies, looking at his laptop screen just as he gets a message on his phone from Rupert asking Joe to ring him. Joe goes out to the back garden to ring Rupert.

"Rupert," Joe says, with the phone to his ear.

Rupert is in the local gym covered in sweat, in the middle of an early morning session.

"I got something for you. Come over to my house about 11am" he tells Joe, before putting down the phone and continuing his gym session.

Joe walks back into the house and goes upstairs to get ready to go and meet Rupert. April is taking the kids to school and the kids call upstairs, "BYE DADDY" to Joe.

They leave as Joe is rushing to go and see Rupert.

City of London...

Kirsty arrives in the busy city for a day of hard work while Ray is at home, lying in bed, smoking a spliff.

In Brixton...

Troy is getting a morning massage from one of his girlfriends while he sits at his desk, now waiting for Joe to come running.

Little John has just picked up his daily newspaper from the local shop and is sitting in his car looking on his phone at Joe's online business. It was not a good day's business as Joe's tips all lost for the first time and the business had a loss. Maybe the stress of all of what is going on is making it harder for Joe to focus.

11:02am...

Joe arrives at Rupert's.

Rupert takes Joe through the extended back of Rupert's house to his studio and office to show Joe what he has on the lock up burglary.

Opening the door to his dark office, Rupert walks straight in and towards his computer monitor screen, he gets up a CCTV camera image.

"Think you might want a look at this bruv" Rupert says to Joe who is still standing by the door, he walks over to have a look for himself.

Rupert clicks the computer mouse and gets up a photo of the pocket watch taken from Joe's lock up.

"Is this your pocket watch, your grandfather's?" Rupert asks Joe.

Joe, looking at the screen, "Yeah that's it, that's my grandad's watch!" he declares.

Rupert clicks back onto the CCTV image of the Lad in the pawn shop and Joe looks closer at the screen to see who it is who sold the pocket watch.

"You know this fool?" Rupert asks, both staring at the CCTV image.

Joe scrutinises the image.

"Yeah, that's one of them Lads from around the estate" Joe says as he recognises the Lad on the CCTV image.

Rupert turns his head towards Joe,

"Luckily, I know every shop owner around this part of town. My guy has put the watch back and you can go collect it when you're ready."

Rupert says, walking away and leaving Joe looking at the computer screen.

Joe is thinking about how to deal with this,

"What am I going to do about this Rupert?" Joe asks Rupert who is now pouring himself a pineapple spiced rum. He turns back around towards Joe,

"About Troy's missing parcel? I think you need to find out who really took it. Maybe starting with that Lad who took the watch" Rupert replies, before asking Joe,

"You want a rum?"

Joe declines the drink offer,

"Nah, not for me mate. Bit early ain't it?" he says before Rupert turns around leaving the room with Joe following.

Ray is still at home, now watching the television highlights from Sunday's FA cup semi-finals on the sofa, slightly stoned from the two spliffs he has already smoked this morning.

He has just watched the highlights of the other football match, Everton v Manchester United.

It was time for the Watford v Crystal Palace match which Ray had had tickets for, but he couldn't make because it fell on the same day as his and girlfriend Kirsty's anniversary. He is now thinking about how he will be going to the club's biggest football match in 26 years, a repeat of that 1990 final between Crystal Palace and Manchester United with all the build-up, when the TV presenter says,

"And now for the other semi-final, where the winner will play Manchester United in the final on May 21st".

Ray, smiling up to this point, knowing that the presenter is talking about Crystal Palace making it to the final, but his face drops after hearing the date... May 21st it stuck out straight away.

It should do too, it's Kirsty's birthday! Ray can't believe his luck and his face says it all.

Back at Rupert's...

Joe thanks Rupert for tracking down his pocket watch and Rupert tells Joe, "I will call in a favour to try and sort this out. I'll be in touch." They nudge fists and Joe leaves now knowing that at least he can get his sentimental pocket watch back.

A little later in the afternoon...

Little John arrives at Troy's house for a daily update on their venture and the current issue of Joe.

John sits across from Troy who is getting his shoulders massaged by one of his girlfriends.

"So, when do you want me to make the call Boss?" asks John.

Troy pauses in thought and says,

"Leave it at least another day, I want to see if he is going to call me or try replace it or pay for it."

"It wouldn't be the end of the world if Joe didn't work for us anymore, the Lads can replace him. Getting a big enough pay out from him might be the wiser option."

"If he wants to leave, he will leave anyway. So, let's see. It's £60,000 he owes if the parcel don't come back as ours. Which it ain't as we already have it." says Troy.

Little John smiling, replies,

"So, Joe is pretty fucked either way then".

In the City of London...

Kirsty has just finished work and is on her way home to Ray, who is still in a state of shock, feeling like he is the unluckiest football fan going right now.

Kirsty comes through the front door and finds Ray sitting in the living room looking down in the dumps.

"What's up with you?" she asks Ray.

Ray looks up at Kirsty and asks,

"What are you doing for your birthday babe?"

Kirsty looks at him and smiles, thinking Ray is planning something to make up for the anniversary.

"Nothing yet, why what are you thinking?"

Ray looks down at the floor and then back at Kirsty who takes a second to realise it might have something to do with football again. She drops the smile and walks away with a fed-up look, shaking her head.

WEDNESDAY, 27th APRIL...

Today Little John is planning to make the call about Troy's missing parcel that Joe is dreading. But Joe has found out who was behind the break-in, the Lads from the estate.

Joe doesn't know for sure though and doesn't have any proof apart from the CCTV image Rupert was able to get, of one of the Lads with his pocket watch.

Ray's mate Billy, along with the Lads, Troy and Little John are all in the frame.

Rupert has called on that favour from an extremely dangerous, and very well-equipped, old friend, 'Jag Jigger'.

Jag has been asked to help with the situation of the break-in at the lock up and the missing parcel, hopefully before Joe gets that call.

9:16am, Joe's house...

With April out doing the usual daily school run, Joe is home alone waiting for the phone to ring... literally.

With Little John calling to pick up Troy's parcel any day, Joe is waiting to see what Rupert is going to do. Joe sits at his laptop at the kitchen island, on the screen is Joe's online business latest summary and it's not good. Joe has taken his eye off the ball slightly, with everything going on, and as a result has possibly had a bit of a desperate mind set, which in the gambling world is a big no.

No wins to shout about, no positive comments and no profit, just a loss.

Joe stares at the laptop deep in thought. He keeps looking at his phone as if he knows it is going to ring... and then it does.

His face pulls still, and his hand moves closer to the phone ringing in front of him. Nervously, he picks it up to see who is calling.

Joe answers the phone... "RAY"

Ray is lying in bed at home and has phoned Joe to confirm Joe's request.

"Morning bro, just to let you know before I forget. I spoke to Billy last night, he is adamant he knows nothing about the lock up break-in. But I got him to meet us as you asked. He is coming tomorrow night" Ray says to Joe.

Joe replies,

"Yeah, I got a feeling I know who is behind it. Tell him not to worry to come up here. If I find out it is him, I will come to Brighton myself".

Ray looks slightly confused, as usual,

"Who do you think it is bro?" Ray asks.

"I'll tell you when I find out" replies Joe.

Ray then says,

"Oh yeah, that's another thing. I thought this tip site you have is profitable. I done your free tip yesterday".

Joe looks at his laptop, slightly fed up and says,

"I know, my head ain't exactly been with it lately, has it? Anyway, what are you doing gambling?" Joe asks.

"Well with all the rave about it, I thought I would have a go" Ray replies.

Joe shakes his head with disapproval and disbelief, with everything else going on.

10:22am, Troy's house...

Troy is sitting at his desk drinking coffee, he picks up his phone and puts it to his ear to make a call to Little John.

"Today is the day John, make the call. Let's get this show on the road" says Troy with a serious look on his face.

Little John is at home sitting on his sofa, he nods and tells Troy, "I will keep you updated, Boss".

11:58am, Rupert's industrial unit, Brixton...

Rupert is with his old friend Jag in the back room of his large unit. The computer screen is on, and they are looking at the CCTV images sent over from the pawn shop owner of the Lad selling the watch. Jag takes a photo of the Lad on his phone after Rupert has zoomed in on his face. Rupert gives Jag a piece of paper with the Lad Jayson's address on it.

The Lad in question is currently only just lifting his head from his bed in his rubbish cluttered bedroom which is scattered with dirty washing and drug paraphernalia. He has no idea what today has in store for him, he thinks he got away with the little extra by not declaring to the other Lads that he had the watch and selling it in the pawn shop for straight up cash behind their backs.

Back at Little John's...

John is about to make the call to Joe to arrange collection of the parcel he only dropped to him less than a week ago. Joe has left his house and is setting off to go to the Lad Jayson's home address given on the pawn shop receipt. First though, he pays the shop owner the £350 he forked out plus a drink on top for calling Rupert. It is worth it to get the pocket watch back that means so much to him. While in the pawn shop finalising the payment, Joe's phone starts ringing.

Joe takes his phone out of his pocket and sees it's Little John ringing. He pauses in thought for a couple of seconds and silences the ringing volume, ignoring the call for now.

John is sitting in his car looking unimpressed by Joe not answering the phone, he texts him, 'CALL ME'

He opens his glove box and gets out the envelope containing photos of April and Denny at football the previous Sunday.

Shortly after...

Joe gets to the address given on the pawn shop receipt and knocks on the door.

The Lad, Jay, has only been awake less than an hour and is smoking a spliff in bed when he hears a knock on the door.

He casually gets up and off his bed to walk out of his bedroom, mumbling to himself,

"Better not be a fucking delivery for next door".

He peeps through the door spy hole and sees Joe standing on the other side. He freezes with shock, slowly tiptoeing away from the door and back into his room. With a worried look on his face he shuts his bedroom door behind him.

Joe waits about a minute and with no answer then leaves and heads home.

On route…

Little John drives around the corner and notices Joe is walking down the street. He pulls up beside Joe.

"I called you earlier, everything alright?" John says leaning over in the driver's seat to talk to Joe who is standing on the pavement.

Joe gets in Little John's car, puts his head down and tells John,

"No, not really, I have sort of misplaced your parcel. well someone has nicked it" he looks at John with a worried look on his face.

"Well, do you know who?" Little John says to Joe.

"I think it's one of them lads from around the estate" Joe says to John looking to see his reaction.

"What makes you think that?" John asks Joe casually, trying not to show any emotions.

Joe thinks he notices a split-second reaction from John and just replies, "I just have a feeling".

John then quickly turns his attitude aggressive to tell Joe, "Well what has happened and who ever done it has nothing to do with me or, more importantly, Troy"

Joe, sitting in the passenger seat replies "Give me a few days, I'll sort it".

Little John stops Joe talking, raising his voice,

"No! Troy ain't got a few days. I will let you know what Troy says".

"Now get out of my car" he tells Joe.

Joe, shocked, looks at John and pauses… he then gets out of the car and John speeds off. Joe watches him drive away, now thinking Little John and Troy might be behind the whole thing.

A bit later that evening…

7:07pm…

Jag pulls up in his car across the road from the Lad Jay's address that Rupert gave him earlier, the same address Joe tried only a few hours ago.

Tinted windows up and engine off, Jag waits across the road with the photo of the Lad Rupert gave him in his hand.

Little John is now over at Troy's telling Troy what Joe has told him and how he might have found out who is behind the break-in of his lock up.

Troy, sitting at his desk across from Little John, is not happy.

"How the fuck does he know who broke in? Them stupid lads" says Troy, looking angrily at John.

Little John replies,

"He doesn't, he just has a feeling. He knows nothing."

"So, what now Boss?" John asks.

"It's sixty grand needed or he will have to work it off. I don't care what he thinks he knows. I want my parcel back, payment in full or he stays on." Troy says as Little John nods his understanding and agreement.

CHAPTER SIX
GOING UNDERGROUND

The next day...

Jag waited just across the road from Jay's house all evening in his car, with no sign of the Lad coming in or out of the address given. Jag has now returned to carry on waiting for a sign of Jayson, and his persistence has paid off. Jayson comes out of his house, looking sheepish, he glances around as he walks 50 yards down the road to meet a kid to pick up a small bag of weed. Jag grabs his opportunity and gets out of the car, walking towards the Lad who is now walking back to his house and turning into his front garden, pulling his keys out of pocket. Jag is only feet away from him now.

The Lad gets to his front door and just as he is about to put the key into the lock, he feels something gently poke his shoulder from behind. He freezes then turns around slowly to see Jag standing in front of him pressing a gun into his chest.

"You need to come with me, and I'd rather take you alive" Jag says to the Lad as he grabs his arm and escorts him back out onto the street and towards his car.

The Lad, who doesn't know who Jag is or why he is taking him, tries to plead with Jag.

"Mate what is this about?" he asks, as they approach the car.

Jag escorts the Lad to the car parked just across the road.

"Get in" Jag demands the Lad. The Lad looks at Jag now shaking with nerves but gets in Jag's car before Jag gets in beside him.

"Where are we going?" The Lad sitting in the passenger seat asks Jag who drives just over a mile away before pulling into an old warehouse on an industrial estate, Rupert's industrial estate.

At Joe and April's...

Joe is on the sofa with April cuddled up with him watching TV.

While at Rupert's...

Rupert tells Rose he is popping out, Rose looks at the clock and turns to Rupert.

"Where are you going at this sort of time?"

Joe is lying on the sofa with April on top of him both watching TV when Joe's phone rings.

"At this time of night on a Wednesday?" April says referring to people wanting drugs. Joe picks his phone up from the table in front of them and looks at it. April is still lying on top of him.

"It's Rupert" Joe says, before answering the phone.

At Rupert's warehouse...

Rupert is standing in his warehouse on the dark and quiet industrial estate. The Lad Jay is blindfolded and tied to a chair in the middle of the room, with Jag standing next to him holding his gun. The Lad begs Jag to let him go, Jag puts the gun to the Lad's head and tells him,

"Be quiet"

Rupert is on the phone to Joe,

"I got our little friend who had your watch..."

"Get yourself down here" he tells Joe.

Joe moves April off him and tells her he needs to go out to sort something out with Rupert.

April sulks as she was so comfortable lying on him and not impressed that he must go out at this time.

"Don't be long please and be careful, whatever you're doing." she says as Joe leaves the room to grab his coat and put his shoes on.

11 minutes later...

The Lad, Jayson is still tied to the chair and blindfolded when Jag, standing behind him, pulls the blindfold up. Jayson's eyes are squinting, having been blindfolded for the last 40 minutes.

When his eyes start to focus, in front of his face is the pocket watch being swung gently from side to side by Joe.

"Hello mate" Joe says to the Lad, Jay.

"You recognise this?" he asks, smiling.

Jayson shits himself straight away and tells Joe everything, that Little John and Troy ordered the Lads to watch Joe collect the parcel from Little John, follow him and nick the parcel back. He said they were allowed to keep anything else that was in there plus they were getting paid by little John for the break in. But that's all he knows, he tells Joe, he doesn't know why Little John asked them to do this to Joe.

Joe turns to Rupert who is standing in a dark corner of the room.

"Bro, I told you about that Troy" Rupert says to Joe.

Joe looks deep in thought about what to do now.

Meanwhile, Ray's mate Billy is driving in his car, just coming into London. He is on route to meet Ray and Joe at the underground car park because Ray has forgotten to let him know that he didn't need to come. Especially now Joe knows for sure it was nothing to do with Billy.

Ray is at home on his balcony smoking a spliff while Kirsty is getting ready for bed. He has no idea what is going on less than a mile away in his uncle's industrial warehouse.

At the warehouse...

Joe has a plan, he walks towards the Lad, still tied up to the chair and asks him, "Have you got your phone on you?"

The Lad replies sheepishly, "Yeah, why?"

"I take it you have John's number then?" Joe asks Jayson.

"I want you to phone Little John and tell him you have a cash buyer for a key of coke. Tonight."

"Any funny business from you and my pal here will take you out of here and drop you in the Thames. Understood?" he says, looking at him while going through the Lad's pocket to get his phone out.

Jag unties Jayson so he can make the phone call to Little John. Rupert looks confused, not knowing what Joe has just thought of.

Little John is still at Troy's, just about to leave, as he is getting up out of the chair, his phone rings.

Little John answers his phone,

"You lot do work late, don't you? What are you, fucking vampires?" John says as he answers the phone, before pausing to listen.

"When, tonight? Nah it's too late now, tell them tomorrow" he listens to what the Lad says.

"One second" says John as he turns to Troy.

"One of our Lads got a buyer for Joe's parcel, cash...but now" John says to Troy.

Troy thinks for a second and then nods to call the deal on.

Little John turns back to the phone call, "you sure they got the money? £50k?"

The Lad, on the phone in the warehouse with Joe, Rupert and Jag holding a gun towards him,

"Yeah, they got it" he says to John on the phone.

Joe hears the price of fifty grand knowing Troy is charging him ten grand more, mutters under his breath, "cheeky cunt".

Little John is still at Troy's, on the phone.

"Usual place, one hour" Little John says to the Lad, before turning back towards Troy and smiling. Troy ponders the value of the phone call,

"These Lads of yours seem to be quite handy" Troy says to John.

Back in the warehouse...

Joe phones Ray after hearing the details of where and when to meet Little John, aware it isn't as genuine as John and Troy think.

Ray is sitting watching television in his living room, Kirsty has gone to bed, when his phone rings.

"Easy, bro" Ray says, answering the phone to Joe.

Joe tells Ray to meet him at his lock up in 20 minutes. Ray gets on his coat and leaves the house quickly. Kirsty, not yet asleep, comes out of the bedroom hearing the front door close to find Ray has left the house. He has left the TV on and a plate of half-eaten food on the sofa.

The underground car park, Brixton...

Billy pulls up to the car park as he has been asked to by Ray, unaware that he has driven all this way for nothing.

While in the warehouse...

Joe tells Jag he will ring him in twenty minutes and to keep the Lad there. Jag ties the Lad's hands together and his ankles to the chair before Joe and Rupert leave the warehouse. As he leaves, Rupert asks,

"Joe, what are you doing?"

Rupert is still unaware of Joe's plan.

Joe replies,

"Killing two birds with one stone, hopefully" They both leave, Rupert is going back home to wife Rose and tells Joe to clean up and lock up when he is done in his warehouse.

Joe goes home quickly, sneaking in quietly as April has fallen asleep on the sofa with the TV still on. He goes straight upstairs and grabs the fake banknotes from the top of the cupboard and puts them into a bag. He comes back down the stairs and leaves quietly after kissing April on her head as she sleeps on the sofa. He leaves the house and heads to the lock up to meet Ray with the bag of fake notes in hand.

At Troy's...

Troy tells Little John he wants to come with him to oversee the deal and meet this Lad. Troy now has big plans for him after the Lads successfully got Troy's parcel back, and he has a cash buyer which could solve the problem of Joe leaving.

Meanwhile at Joe's lock up...

Joe meets Ray at the lock up so Joe can put the notes into a sports bag. He puts in £45,000 of fake notes and £5,000 of his own real money to top it up to the £50,000 needed in total and zips the bag back up.

"Charges me sixty but this little cunt fifty, what a wanker" Joe says to himself about Troy's price and then puts back the other £20,000 of fake notes, in the safe this time based on previous experience.

Ray totally and rightfully confused at this point, watching what Joe is doing asks,

"What the hell you are doing bro?"

Ray is also still unaware of anything that is going on.

Joe makes a call to Jag to meet him outside his lock up.

Little John and Troy are about to leave when Troy hands Little John a bag with the same parcel that was taken from Joe's. Little John puts the bag in the car boot, Troy gets in the back seat and Little John gets in the driving seat. They make their way to the meeting stop, the underground car park.

Billy is still waiting for Ray and Joe to show up and tries to ring Ray.

With no answer, Billy leaves a voice message,

"Yeah ray, it's billy, I am here waiting mate." He sits in his car looking around the car park.

Joe's lock up...

Joe and Ray leave Joe's lock up, shutting and locking up before Joe stands and waits with Ray still not having a clue what is going on. Jag, with the Lad in the back of his car, pulls up outside Joe's lock up where Joe and Ray are waiting outside. Joe walks up to Jag's car and hands the bag of banknotes to Jag. Jag nods at Joe, puts the bag on the passenger seat and drives off.

Ray standing next to Joe with his usual bewildered look on his face asks Joe,

"What the fuck is going on?"

Joe watches Jag drive off then turns to Ray and asks,

"Got any weed on you?" and walks off, Ray even more confused follows Joe.

Jag's car...

On route to the underground car park, the Lad sends a sneaky text, without Jag seeing, to the other Lads to come and help him, telling them to 'COME UNDERGROUND CAR PARK QUICK'.

As soon as one of the Lads gets this message the three Lads gather up and tool up with a knife and a baseball bat and head for the underground car park.

Little John and Troy pull into the underground car park and park the car. They wait for the Lad Jay and Jag, who is the supposed buyer of the parcel that Little John and Troy are bringing.

Jag pulls into the underground car park and gives the orders to the Lad sitting in the back seat, "Just play along with this and you will be in the clear, OK? we will even pay you. Remember I know where you and your family live" Jag says.

The Lad nods nervously to Jag.

"Now just give the bag to your guy and take the parcel, get back in the car and I take you home with no drama" Jag says.

"OK no problem, I will do that. But then you take me home, yeah?" the agitated Lad replies as they pull up next to Troy and Little John waiting in the car.

It's at this time that the other three Lads are also approaching the underground carpark after getting the SOS text message. On approaching the entrance, the Lads pull their tools out from underneath their clothes and are seen by a couple of members of the local community who are on their way back from bingo. The ladies are already aware of the Lads from the estate and know they are trouble. On seeing the Lads with weapons, heading towards the entrance of the underground car park, one of the ladies pulls her phone out and rings the police.

"Police please... The underground car park, Brixton..."

"There is three lads with weapons, quick" she says to the operator on the phone, watching as the Lads enter the car park.

Brixton canal...

Joe and Ray are sitting on a bench overlooking Brixton and the city of London skyline. Ray has just rolled a spliff, he lights it up, takes a few puffs and then passes it to Joe.

"I still don't know what is going on" Ray says as he watches Joe puff on the spliff.

Joe says with smoke in his throat,

"Hopefully it's all over soon, no more Troy or Little John, Billy or any other dodgy fucker... Apart from you" He looks at Ray smiling.

Ray suddenly remembers he forgot to do something.

"Billy... fuck!" he says,

"I forgot to tell him not to drive down."

He pulls his phone out of his pocket to look at it.

"Yeah, he has phoned me..."

"He will be waiting in the underground car park for us" he says as Joe passes the spliff back to him.

Joe looks at Ray,

"The underground car park?" knowing that Jag and the Lad Jay are meeting Little John there.

Back in the underground car park...

Billy is getting fed up with waiting and lights up one last cigarette before he decides to leave, unaware anyone else is in the car park.

Jag orders the Lad to hand Little John the bag of cash as the Lad gets out of the car with the bag and walks over to Little John with Jag behind him. John takes the bag, has a quick look inside and passes it through the car window to Troy to check if the cash is right. Out of nowhere police sirens can be heard coming closer and blue flashing lights approaching the underground car park.

Jag grabs the Lad and throws him back into the car before quickly getting in and driving away from the oncoming police cars screaming into the car park entrance.

Little John runs around his car with Troy in the back seat checking the bag of cash, the parcel of coke is still in the boot. John grabs the bag and slams the boot closed. He drops the bag on the floor and tries to kick it under a parked car before jumping in his car and speeding off.

At that very moment Billy flicks his cigarette out of the window and starts the engine, pulling away and out of the parking bay he has been waiting in the last hour. When he drives out, he happens to block Little John and Troy from getting out of the car park. The police are speeding up behind John and Troy's car. The other Lads who were wandering around the car park looking for their mate, have run away from the scene which is now covered with police.

Brixton canal...

Ray is still sitting on the park bench and refers to Billy,

"Ah, he will be gone and on his way home now"

He lights up his spliff with Joe wondering what on earth might be happening right now.

Underground car park...

Billy panics and stalls the car, thinking the police might be coming for him so just closes his eyes for a couple of seconds. When he opens them, he sees the police pointing guns and screaming at Little John and Troy to step out of the car with their hands on their head.

Billy realises he is in the clear and slowly drives away looking in his back mirror at the police bundling Little John and Troy out of their car.

On the way out of the underground car park, Billy spots the bag on the floor next to the car that Little John dropped it by. Looking around to see if anyone is near, Billy quickly jumps out and grabs the bag before throwing it on the passenger seat and getting out of there as quickly as he can before getting pulled by the police.

On the bench...

Ray puts his phone in his pocket and continues to smoke his spliff with Joe.

Little John and Troy have just been arrested with the bag containing mainly fake banknotes and are taken to the police station.

Billy pulls over down the road after getting out of the underground car park with the bag. He stops to have a look. Billy unzips the bag to find a large parcel inside, pulling it out to investigate, he rips a little hole in the parcel, pokes his finger in the hole and then rubs his finger on his gum.

Billy's eyes light up, but with the sound of police cars everywhere and the situation back at the underground car park, Billy decides it's best to get out of there. He places the parcel back in the bag and drives off as normally as possible back to Brighton.

Meanwhile, Jag is racing through the streets of London to get to the docks with the Lad. He parks up near the edge of River Thames and orders the Lad out of the car.

"I thought you were taking me home," Jayson says to Jag who is about eight feet away. He turns around to face Jag who is pointing a gun towards him. Jag shoots him twice in the chest and then rolls his body off the edge into the river.

Brixton police station...

Troy and Little John get brought into the police station for questioning and in the interview room the police officer asks them,

"So, any reason you had £50,000 in mainly fake banknotes?"

Troy looks confused, then realising he must have been set up, replies,

"No comment" to the officer interviewing him.

Three weeks later...

SATURDAY 21st MAY 2016...

South London is buzzing because Crystal Palace are playing in the FA cup final against Manchester United on the north side of the river, at Wembley stadium this afternoon.

It's also Kirsty's birthday.

Last week Troy and Little John were in court for sentencing. Troy got nine months for handling counterfeit banknotes with intention to use them. Little John got two months for driving away, aiding Troy. Little John will be back out and free in a couple weeks on good behaviour, but Troy won't be free for at least another three to four months, depending on his behaviour of course.

Back in South London...

After hearing Ray go on about nothing else but the big FA cup final, Kirsty agrees to go to the football match with him, and thousands of south Londoners, on the condition he takes her on holiday soon after.

In the end, Kirsty really enjoyed herself, being in the crowd and singing the songs while they both drank pints of beer from plastic cups in the sun at Wembley stadium.

Joe watches the match at home with April on the sofa. Safe in the knowledge that Troy will be away for a while and Rupert's mate Jag dealt with the Lad. There should be no comebacks on where the banknotes came from as the Lad is now at the bottom of the river Thames somewhere.

Two weeks later...

SATURDAY, 7TH JUNE 2016...

Summer is fast approaching. There is already the feel of the heat and the sunshine hot weather vibe in the air.

Joe and Ray are in Joe's lock up with the door open and shutters up. Joe is cleaning and clearing it out as he has no real use for it now and is not renewing the lease.

Ray is supposed to be helping, standing there smoking a spliff talking about how mad it is that Leicester City are champions of England having won the Premier league a few weeks ago at a starting betting odds of 2000/1.

"Bro, shame you did not have Leicester on your online business" Ray says before changing the subject.

Word on the street is that Troy was attacked in prison and died. Insiders say they saw Troy lying in his cell in a pool of blood.

Ray asks Joe,

"So, you going to tell me what happened with Troy. The break in and all that?"

Joe proceeds to explain what he knows regarding the situation and how he used the banknotes from Billy to set up a meeting with John to get the parcel back.

But unexpectedly the police came screaming in and arrested him and Troy. He explains that Jag took the Lad and dealt with him as he was going to anyway.

Joe goes on to say that Troy has been done over in prison and his body has been shipped away back to his motherland, Turkey for a quick burial. So, no Troy means no debt and it has all been finally cleaned up as the Lad used as bait has gone.

Ray looks totally shocked with all that Joe just told him," Troy's dead? Fucking hell!"

Joe looks at Ray and then says, "So, it's over, I hope".

Ray then thinks, "What about John?" he says, looking slightly confused again.

Joe replies,

"Fuck knows, but he ain't got Troy now, has he? So, it don't matter"

Down in Brighton...

Billy still has the parcel he found in the underground car park and has decided to try a bit more of the class A drug. He dabs some on his finger and onto his tongue. His eyes light up and he places a small pile onto a CD case. He starts lining up before wrapping up the bag containing the kilo, minus a few grams now, zipping it closed and putting on the side.

At the lock up...

A car pulls up outside Joe's garage. Little John steps out of the driver's door and walks around the car.

Joe looks at Ray and says,

"I told you, you were a jinx"

He watches Little John open the back passenger door for a rather large looking version of Troy. The guy walks over to Joe and Ray who are just inside the lock up and says,

" I'm Chase, Troy's brother."

"I hear you have something of my brother's, £60k was it not?" he says to Joe, Little John beside him smirking.

Joe shakes his head then replies,

"One minute, I need to make a phone call".

Joe takes his phone out and walks to the back of his lock up.

"Alright mate? I got Troy's brother here demanding £60k" Joe says holding the phone to his ear before he walks from the back of the lock up to Chase and says,

"Saturday night, I will give John details on where to meet. I need to go and grab it obviously".

Chase looks at Joe with a serious look on his face but accepts the terms for gathering such a large sum of cash.

Over at Rupert's...

Rupert has just got off the phone, wife Rose is standing over him intrigued as to what Rupert is up to now.

Rupert looks at Rose and smiles, but as Rose walks away Rupert's smile drops. He picks up his phone to make a call without Rose hearing.

At the lock up...

Chase and Little John get back in their car and drive off.

Joe looks at Ray, who looks confused. Joe watches Little John drive off with Chase. He can't believe he again has the problem of the £60,000 debt along with Little John, and Troy's bigger brother to deal with. Just when he thought he got away clean. Ray's phone rings.

He answers, "Yeah, what's up Bill?"

Rays listens to Billy on the phone and his face drops in shock.

"You got what?" asks Ray.

Ray looks at Joe and Joe says,

"No, I don't want anything, thank you."

He puts his hand up to stop Ray asking, assuming it's more knocked off or fake stuff like usual.

Billy on the phone to Ray is now slumped in his chair with his jaw swinging and tells Ray,

"Yeah, and it's the real thing. I need to get rid of this or I'll die man!"

Ray speaks to Joe still holding the phone to his ear,

"Joe, he's got a big bag of coke he found couple weeks back".

Billy sends Ray a photo of the bag. Ray's eyes light up when he sees the photo.

"You better look at this bro," Ray tells Joe.

Joe walks over to Ray.

Joe looks confused and takes the phone to investigate the photo.

"Oh my god" says Joe looking at the photo.

Ray asks, "Isn't that your bag?"

Joe replies, "It is indeed".

He stares at the photo on the phone screen deep in thought about what to do next.

CHAPTER SEVEN

RIVERS N FLAGS

THURSDAY, 9TH JUNE 2016…

Joe's lock up…

Billy pulls into Joe's lock up after driving up from Brighton with the parcel.

Joe and Ray are standing there in wait as Billy pulls up and gets out of the car, greeting Joe and Ray,

"Hello again lads" says Billy, smiling at Joe and Ray.

"Easy Bill, again sorry about not letting you know you did not have to drive down that time" says Ray smiling back.

Joe looks at Billy and then Ray.

"That's alright Ray, seems it was worth it now" Billy replies before Ray asks,

"So, what ya been up to then Bill?"

Joe looks confused and then fed up with Ray,

"What's this? A fucking mother's meeting? Come on Bill, show me what you got." Joe says walking towards Bill who is standing at the boot of his car.

Billy opens the boot.

Elsewhere...

The rest of the country are getting ready for the Brexit vote result in a couple of weeks but before that it's England v Wales in the Euros.

Back at Joe's Lock up...

Joe is standing looking at the slightly unzipped bag of cocaine in the boot of Billy's car,

"How much Billy?" Joe asks, opening the bag more to inspect.

"I only done about two grams. I still ain't slept" Billy says, giggling.

"I wouldn't of stopped though with that much. I would just die man, ya know?"

"Thing is, it might be from someone you know as I found it close by" Billy then tells Joe and Ray.

Ray smiles at Billy and Joe says,

"Yeah, don't worry, we know whose it is."

Billy, panicking slightly, declares,

"Oh well, I found it honestly."

He is worried he may be in trouble.

Joe wants to get this done quickly,

"Five grand" he says, turning to look at Billy.

Billy thinking, replies "Ten"

Joe frowns at Billy and bids again, "Six" he says.

"Eight" Billy offers.

Joe is getting fed up now,

"OK seven then, £7k Bill. I really ain't in the mood to fuck around, take the seven and be grateful you get that. As I said, I do know who this parcel belongs to, and he will not give you seven."

He says pulling out a small, padded envelope filled with £50 notes. He takes £3000 out of the bundle of cash, placing it in his inside coat pocket and hands Billy the envelope containing £7000 cash.

"Well, nice doing business with you again lads" Billy says as he hands Joe the bag and closes the boot of his car.

Joe, looking down at the bag he is holding, is still amazed how it has come back into his hands after going missing and all the drama it has caused.

As Billy gets in the car he says to Joe and Ray, "Just lucky when I pulled out and got that geezer nicked, he did not have it, as it must have been something to do with that".

Joe clocks what Billy has just said,

"What geezer?" Joe asks Billy who is about to jump in his car.

Billy stands back up beside his car.

"Don't know, I just see a big silver car I pulled out on and stalled the car, then a few seconds later the police, sirens, the lot. So it might have been my fault. Oh shit, you said you knew him." Billy says with a worried look realising he might have just put his foot in it.

Joe smiles with content, takes the £3000 out of his pocket and hands it across to Billy. Now both Billy and Ray look confused.

"Nah, you might of actually done me a favour" Joe says.

Billy takes the cash with a smile,

"Cool man" he says before getting back in his car to leave.

Ray and Joe look at each other and smile. Joe is holding the bag containing the cocaine that is worth around £50,000. Chase is expecting Troy's parcel back and now, somehow, Joe luckily has it back in his hands. So, there shouldn't be any problems now... hopefully.

FRIDAY, 10TH JUNE 2016...

TILBURY DOCKS, ESSEX

This morning, a body has been washed up on the banks of the river Thames in Essex just short of the English Channel. The police named the 26-year-old as Jayson Bridle of Brixton.

It's the Lad Jag shot and dumped in the river near Greenwich over six weeks ago. The story has been in all the local newspapers and news programmes.

Jag now has another job, to meet Troy's brother Chase at the docks tomorrow night. He will take care of Chase in the same way he did the Lad Jay if Chase won't take the parcel back. That will finally end the affairs about the £60,000 debt owed. Joe knows Troy was behind it to keep him in his pocket, but this must be the end now.

Meanwhile…

Ray is at home sitting in his living room in his Wales football team shirt, Welsh flags on the wall along with a Jamaican flag and one little England flag.

He is watching the opening ceremony of the 2016 European championships, (Euro2016) the first match is the host, France playing Romania.

Kirsty walks into the room, seeing the living room decorated with flags and Ray sitting there in his Welsh kit.

"What on earth is going on here?" Kirsty asks, looking around the room at the flags.

Ray, eyes glued to the television, replies,

"Euros babe"

Kirsty looks at him with confusion and replies "oh right"

Seeing the Jamaican flag Kirsty asks,

"If it's the euros, why are Jamaica in it? Jamaica ain't in Europe!"

Ray replies, eyes still glued to the tele,

"Nah they are not, not in the Euros."

Kirsty looks even more confused,

"So why is there a Jamaican flag on the wall? There ain't even any England flags" she says to Ray.

Ray points out the little England flag in the corner and says,

"There you go. I am Jamaican and Welsh, then English."

Kirsty looks at Ray and the television showing the opening ceremony and says,

"What's this? this ain't football."

Ray is glued to the television,

"It's the opening ceremony babe" he replies getting annoyed with all the questions.

"So, who is Wales playing now then?" Kirsty asks.

Ray looks at Kirsty to explain,

"Slovakia, tomorrow 5PM"

"France are playing Romania soon" he says.

Kirsty replies, looking no less confused than before,

"So why are you sitting there in your Wales top now?" She shakes her head and leaves the room, leaving Ray watching the tele, in his element.

Over at Joe's...

April is getting the house all tidy while the kids are at school. She is packing suitcases for their family holiday in Cornwall in a couple of days.

Joe is at his laptop screen working away when April walks up to him with news she just heard on social media.

"Babe did you hear about that body they pulled from the Thames in Essex?"

"It was one of them young lads from the estate, mental!"

Joe's face changes to shock at the news, but without April noticing and decides to take a break and pop to the shop. He asks April if they need anything before leaving, shutting the front door, and getting straight on the phone to Rupert about what he has just heard.

Rupert is sitting in his home studio.

"Yeah, I heard. Don't worry, just stick to the plan" he tells Joe.

The next day...

Wales are about to play their first major tournament football match in 58 years, playing Slovakia at 5pm. Ray will be ready, in his Wales football shirt, in front of the television cheering them on.

Joe was looking forward to England's opening game of the tournament against Russia at 8pm. But Joe has another date at 8pm tonight. He has a meeting with Troy's brother Chase to give him £60,000 in cash, paying the debt of his, now dead, brother.

News has spread around south London about the missing Lad Jay, being pulled from the river. The other Lads knew something had happened. The last time they heard from him was when he texted asking for help and to come to the underground car park.

The Lads are upset and angry, and of course wanting to seek revenge for their friend.

Ray is getting anxious, but not about the body being washed up that might lead the police back to them. Just anxious because he wants Wales to win the football tonight, the match is starting soon.

But the news is on everyone's television.

The main local headline on the news is that Jayson has been named as the body pulled from the Thames and is awaiting the official autopsy. People will be talking all sorts.

Into the evening...

Ray has just watched his main headline; Wales beat Slovakia 2-1, so he is buzzing and driving Kirsty mad in the process.

Joe is getting ready to meet Chase. He has to go to the lock up to grab a bag for the parcel. The plan is to offer Chase the parcel back as that was what went missing and is owed, technically. Jag will be watching close by in case anything goes wrong.

Over at Little John's...

Little John gives Chase the address to meet Joe, a local warehouse.

He asks Chase if he is alright to go alone and get his cash as England are about to kick off against Russia in their opener of Euro 2016.

"Joe won't give you any grief, you will be more than alright" Little John says standing beside Chase who is sitting in his car.

Chase shakes his head, rolls his eyes and replies,

"Yeah, no problem" before driving off to meet Joe.

7:58pm... Rupert's warehouse, Brixton.

Joe is waiting for Jag to turn up when Chase pulls up into the warehouse. Joe looks anxious as he is now on his own with Chase and doesn't have the £60,000 in cash but instead the parcel that went missing. And no Jag.

If Chase says it's cash only, Joe's fucked.

Chase gets out of the car with Joe standing there holding a sports bag full of cocaine.

Joe passes the bag to Chase who looks inside the bag and then looks at Joe with a confused look.

"What's this?" he asks Joe.

Joe replies, "it's your brother's parcel that he gave me to look after."

Chase isn't impressed and gives the bag back to Joe. He gets up close to his face and tells Joe,

"It's £60,000 cash I am here for."

Out of nowhere, from about 15 feet away from Joe and Chase, they hear, "OI YOU!"

Chase turns towards the voice shouting with an annoyed look on his face before the quiet sound of two quick gunshots firing into the chest of Chase. He falls to the ground right in front of Joe.

Joe, in shock, looks up and sees Jag walking towards him with a pistol in his hand.

"He did not want to settle it fair then, oh well."

Joe looks at Jag with amazement. Jag calmly gets out a cigarette and lights it, both Joe and Jag looking down at Chase, who is dead now too.

"And where have you been?" Joe asks Jag in a sarcastic tone.

"I was waiting for that other div, John. But obviously he came on his jacks. Don't worry son, I had it under control."

Jag replies smoking his fag, looking around for anyone else.

"Go on, go. I'll deal with this" Jag tells Joe.

Joe nods with an unsure look on his face and walks off leaving Jag with Chase's dead body.

The morning after…

It is almost time to leave, April is packing the car that she will be driving for nearly four hours to Cornwall with Joe and the kids.

Joe is still in shock about last night but knows it must be over now as Chase has been eliminated too. But having someone shot dead right in front of him has had a slight effect. Exactly the reason why he wants to get as far away from this world as possible.

April notices that Joe is in a daze.

"Babe, can you at least help me please, I'm packing the car, gotta get the kids ready yet too" she says in a fed-up tone.

Joe snaps out of it and replies,

"Yeah, sorry babe" before helping with kids so they can all leave for a week away in Cornwall.

At Rupert's...

Jag turns up at Rupert's to give him an update. He tells all and Rupert gets straight to the point asking Jag,

"Where did you bury this one? Coz the last one has just washed up in Essex."

He shows Jag a newspaper headline about the Lad's body being found and identified.

Jag in his defence says,

"Well, it all went a bit mental with police turning up. It had to be quick" Rupert listens and nods to agree.

"Yeah, I spose so, just make sure this one ain't found" Rupert tells Jag.

Jag replies with confidence,

"Don't worry, this one is deep. He won't be found."

3 days later…

THURSDAY, 16th JUNE 2016...

Joe, April and the kids have been away in Cornwall for a few days now. Joe needed the break more than ever with everything going on in the last five months or so. Especially as he had Troy's brother shot dead in front of him only days ago. So, he is relaxing on the beach all day with April and the kids, who are loving the seaside, in and out of the sea, building sandcastles. A totally different world to the one they know.

Back in London...

The city is buzzing, like a lot of places up and down the country, as today a fiery encounter is taking place between England and Wales in the second group stage match of the Euro 2016 tournament.

Ray and Kirsty are out in a bar watching the early afternoon kick-off between the two rivals. They are sitting next to each other, Ray in his Wales top and Kirsty sporting an England top. The bar is mixed with both English and Welsh shirts, hats and flags.

Little John is getting concerned about the fact he has not seen or heard from Chase since the meet with Joe. He has made several missed calls and decides to try again, with Chase's phone again going straight through to voicemail. He leaves a message…

"Chase, I am getting worried now, let me know you picked that up or not. And that everything is OK."

Down in Cornwall...

Joe and April decide to go for a walk with the kids to the local beach to play for a few hours. With its clear sea water, golden sand and beautiful view, it is paradise. The kids play in the sea with their

floats and Joe and April walk hand in hand along the beach. Heaven compared to life at home lately.

Looking out to the sea, with its miles of space and the soothing sound of the waves, April says to Joe,

"Can we not move closer to the sea, the beach? This is just bliss."

Joe is also gazing out to sea and replies,

"It would be better than the big shitty city."

He is deep in thought about what life could be like away from South London and all that is going on as they walk along the sandy beach.

The Brexit vote was also decided, with the majority leaning to leave the European Union.

CHAPTER EIGHT
EUROS IN PARIS

4 DAYS LATER...

MONDAY, 20th JUNE 2016...

Joe, April and the kids got back late last night from their week away in Cornwall and it's all go again. April is getting the kids ready for school and Joe is up, ready to deal with what the day brings regarding the body being washed up from the river Thames. The body was recovered just over a week ago now and so far, no news is good news. So, Joe decides to put his phone on silent and have a chilled day and not put himself or others at risk by seeing anyone like Rupert or Ray just in case any of them is being watched.

Joe does, however, have a kilo of coke and £15,000 in fake notes stored in the lock up, this time in a secure, locked, unmovable safe. But still, he needs to get rid of it, especially if the Old Bill are sniffing around and it's possible they could be.

A load of coke possibly carrying the DNA of Jayson, the Lad killed by Jag, on the bag and fake notes is not going to look good.

TUESDAY, 21st JUNE ...

Last night saw both England and Wales going through to the knockout stage of the Euro 2016 football competition. England drew 0-0 against Slovakia in a boring match, and Wales beat Russia 3-0 to top the group. This means Wales's next opponents will be Northern Ireland this coming Saturday in Paris, and England will be playing Iceland in their final last 16 match the Monday after in Nice, France.

Joe has had some good wins of late on his online betting business and is now starting to realise that his problems have gone, no more Troy and no more Chase. And fuck Little John too, the only reason he is still alive is because he wanted to watch the football match rather than escort Chase for safety. Although Joe does have a kilo of cocaine now, he could do with getting rid of it out the way quickly, and them fucking fake banknotes, then that's it.

Over at Ray and Kirsty's...

Ray walks through the door at home where Kirsty is sitting on the sofa going through her paperwork.

"What ya doing baby?" asks Ray.

"Trying to find some old paperwork for my CV, I hate my job and want a new one" replies Kirsty with a fed-up tone.

Ray reaches into his pocket and pulls out an envelope and gives it to Kirsty.

"Well, this might cheer you up" Ray says as he passes the envelope.

Kirsty opens it and looks inside, seeing what's in the envelope she screams with joy and hugs Ray.

"Paris? We're going to Paris? This Saturday!" Kirsty cries out.

She doesn't know that Ray also has tickets for the Wales v Northern Ireland game on Saturday in Paris. He doesn't need to tell Kirsty about that yet.

"Most romantic city baby girl. Or is that Rome?" Ray replies looking confused. This makes Kirsty laugh and seems to have shifted her mood. She throws her arms around Ray and kisses him on the lips, smiling.

Well, until she finds out why they have really gone to Paris.

Word has spread about Troy not being around anymore. The Morris Brothers, George, Glenn and the youngest

Justin from nearby Bermondsey are in the same game, they run the whole of SE1 and SE16 postcode areas. They have heard the rumours and see a great opportunity to expand and take control to fill the void left by Troy's absence.

4 days later…

SATURDAY, 25th JUNE 2016…

10:26am, Waterloo East station…

Ray and Kirsty are about to board a Eurostar train to Paris for a few days away. Kirsty still does not know Ray also has two tickets to the last 16 Euro 2016 match between Wales and Northern Ireland in Paris. He is starting to give it away. Ray has his Wales football shirt on along with many other Welsh fans travelling to Paris to also watch the game. Kick-off is only hours away, Kirsty asks Ray,

"Why is there so many Welsh people around? And why are you in such a hurry?" she looks at Ray, intrigued.

Ray turns to Kirsty with a guilty look on his face.

Kirsty looks horrified,

"No Ray" she says, shaking her head.

"Please tell me this is not about football, I thought we were going to Paris" she says.

Ray replies,

"Babe, Wales are playing in the last 16 against Northern Ireland in Paris, today. We got tickets but we are here for a few days babe"

Kirsty looks fed up but picks her bag up and walks towards the check in desk with Ray smiling in relief. He follows Kirsty towards the desk and they board their train to Paris.

Back in Brixton, South London...

The Morris Brothers (George, Glenn and Justin) approach Joe about working for them now that Troy has gone. Joe is on his way to his lock up and refuses the offer, telling them he is out of that game.

The eldest brother, George, takes out a business card and hands it to Joe.

"Well, if you change your mind…"

Joe takes the card with a phone number on before George gives Joe a wink of the eye and drives away.

In Paris...

Ray and Kirsty are at the football match, which is about to end. Wales are winning 1-0 which means they will go through to the quarter finals the following Friday. Ray is already thinking about going to the quarter final match against Belgium in 6 days' time.

Back in London…

Rupert is working on a project of his own, he has a career in music, making and producing tracks from his home studio. Rose is fully behind the idea, she is happy Rupert is just doing something constructive since quitting the drugs game.

FRIDAY, 1st JUNE...

Wales have made it to the quarter finals of Euro 2016 and play Belgium tonight in the country's biggest football match since a world cup quarter final in 1958. It's their first ever European championship.

Ray is at home sitting in front of the television waiting for the game to start, with his Wales football shirt on and flags still around the living room.

Joe is in his lockup, getting the £15,000 in fake notes out of the safe. He leaves the kilo of cocaine inside, having still not worked out what he is going to do with it. Closing the safe and putting the fake banknotes into a small bag, he leaves the lock up.

In the quarter-finals match, Wales are about to make history and get as far as they ever have before, by beating Belgium 3-1. Ray is ecstatic, jumping around the living room as the full-time whistle goes, he picks up his phone to ring Joe.

Joe, walking back from the lock up, answers his ringing phone,

"Raymondo!" He has to take the phone away from his ear as Ray is shouting with joy about the football.

"I know, what a win! You fancy meeting me by the canal for a celebrational smoke? bring one for me with ya." Joe says to Ray.

With that, Ray grabs his little pouch containing his Rizla papers, tobacco and cannabis. He puts on his coat and leaves the house, leaving the television on. Ray shuts the front door just as Kirsty has woken up from all the noise, she walks into the living room rubbing her eyes,

"Ray, what is all the noise?"

When she takes her hands away from her face Kirsty sees no sign of Ray, "RAY" she calls out.

Joe is waiting by the canal as Ray approaches singing, and still jolly, about Wales winning and making it to the semi-finals of a major tournament.

Rupert is in his studio working hard, finishing production on a track. His wife Rose is happy at home too.

Brixton canal...

Ray pulls out two ready rolled spliffs and hands one to Joe, they both light up and toast to all the good that has happened of late. The success of Wales in the football and the fact they managed to escape from Troy, Little John and Chase.

Joe turns to Ray.

"So, there is just one more thing we need to take care of," he says as he pulls out the fake banknotes and flicks a lighter ready to set fire to them. Ray sees this and tries to stop Joe from setting the wad of cash on fire,

"Bro, what are you doing? We can earn something on that!"

Joe pulls away from Ray, telling him,

"Ray, that lad who has been pulled from the river a few weeks back? Well, his DNA is probably all over these notes. It's not worth the risk mate."

Ray pulls his arm back then watches as Joe sets fire to the stack of banknotes and places them on the ground in front of them, smoking.

Joe again turns to Ray, "And now it is over."

Ray remembers the kilo of cocaine.

"What about your kilo of the devil's dandruff?" Ray asks Joe.

Joe looks across the river deep in thought,

"Yeah, I suppose I better get rid of that too."

Ray looks at Joe, "You're not gonna burn that too, are ya?"

Joe smiles and replies,

"Nah, I can't afford to do that."

They both laugh, now slightly stoned looking down on the burning banknotes.

Wales played Portugal in the semi-finals of Euro 2016, losing 2-0 but Ray is very proud of their effort, and that they got further than England.

Then it all went nice and peaceful, everything was starting to look up. Joe could just get on with his online business while investigating the possibility of moving somewhere near the seaside. No football, no dodgy meetings, no fake banknotes, and no debts.

CHAPTER NINE

RETURN OF THE MACK

FRIDAY, 7th OCTOBER...

Three months go past with no comebacks, leaving everyone to enjoy the rest of the Summer and get ready for the winter months. After the current Autumn season there is the upcoming Halloween party and April's birthday.

Little John is sitting at home watching the horse racing, at a bit of a loss after the demise of Troy and now seemingly Chase too, leaving a void in his life. He is about to get a phone call and the shock of his life.

He is cheering on his horse, screaming at the television to only go and lose.

John's phone rings just as the race is finishing, he picks it up to answer it.

"Oh, for fuck's sake, fucking horses... hello?"

"Hello John"

"Troy... you're alive!" he looks like he has just spoken to a ghost.

Up the country in a west Midlands prison, Troy is using the phone with a small queue of people behind him waiting to use the only prison wing phone. He is speaking to Little John, not dead as thought.

At Joe's...

The kids have been on half term, off school for the week. Both Denny and Izzy are at home baking cakes with April while Joe is at the computer working on his online business.

At the prison...

The phone call comes to an end after Troy asks John, "You got that John?"

John, at home in London replies, "Yes Boss."

He is still in shock that Troy is alive and doesn't know if Chase got Troy's £60,000 from Joe.

At Joe's...

Joe's daughter Izzy brings a few cupcakes on a plate to her dad while he is on the computer. Joe takes the plate, puts it on the side and lifts Izzy up to sit with him for a cuddle. He takes two cupcakes from the plate and gives one to Izzy. They both sit eating cake while Joe continues to work, Izzy chilling with him, happily stuffing her little face with cake with her Daddy.

TUESDAY, 11th OCTOBER...

M42 MOTORWAY, REDDITCH, MIDLANDS...

Little John is driving and singing along to the radio, he turns into the entrance to HMP Hewell Prison, parks up and waits. Looking at the door, waiting for it to open.

Back down in London, Ray has got himself a new job in a restaurant in the west end, training to be a chef. Although it will be mainly washing up and light cooking duties at first until he gets the hang of it.

Meanwhile, Joe checks his bank balance, £83,828.19. He is still on the hunt for a house somewhere out of London.

The business is working, he has put away some savings, paid for holidays and the £10,000 to Billy for the bag of cocaine back. Which he still has and is worth £40,000 easy on a quick sale.

Joe clicks onto an auction site with houses for sale and starts scrolling.

Back at the Prison...

The prison door opens, waking up little John who had fallen asleep after sitting waiting for a couple of hours. John's face lights up at who has just walked out of the prison door. He gets out of the car and walks over towards... Troy, who looks up into the sky and breathes in the air.

"TROY" Little John calls.

He shakes Troy's hand before taking the bag of Troy's belongings for him and escorting him to the car.

"Any sign of my brother?" Troy asks as he lights himself a cigarette.

"Nothing since I gave him the address to meet Joe" John replies.

"Strange" Troy says before they both get into the car.

While driving home Little John asks Troy, who is sitting on the back seat,

"So, how did you do it Boss?"

"Do what John?" replies Troy.

"How did you get out of one prison and up here and have everyone in London think you were dead?" asks John.

Troy explains,

"I had someone on the inside and the screws in my pocket. Made out like I'd been done in and taken to hospital... then put the rumour around I was dead, but I was just moved for my security apparently."

Looking at John, he then says,

"Something ain't right john, your lad with fake notes and then missing, now my brother…"

John intervenes,

"Jay got found washed up in Thames near Essex, it ain't looking good boss... but who?"

Troy turns his head to look at Little John.

"It has to be that Joe. You said he had an idea it was one of the lads, and he was the last person my brother was with" then pausing in thought asks John, "And where were you when chase was meeting Joe?"

Little John looks worried and confesses to Troy,

"It was the big match boss, England."

Troy's face is now turning angry and he gives John a stone-cold look.

"You mean, my brother is missing because you were watching football?" Troy questions John.

John looks even more worried now and pleads to Troy, "Boss, I'm sorry."

Troy thinks about the situation for a few seconds.

"You need to have a meeting with them Lads... this needs to be dealt with" Troy tells John, with John nodding to agree and pulling his phone out to contact the Lads.

Troy then says,

"Oh, and John, remember I am supposed to be dead. I am also gonna have to keep a low profile, take me to Chase's in Croydon."

Little John drives on.

In Brixton...

Joe has just won the online auction bid for the house in Eastbourne, East Sussex, overlooking the sea, for an upfront total payment of £81,000. This is going to clear him out nearly and he will need another £10,000 minimum to refurbish and decorate. Joe really needs to get rid of this parcel now. It would be a perfect send off, with the money helping to finish the house and still leave some for savings, plus he would then, and only then be really out of the game for good.

Troy and Little John arrive at Troy's brother's house in Croydon, there is no sign of anyone at home.

They walk around the back and through the back gate, peering through the windows of darkness when Troy tells Little John,

"Boot the door down John."

John looks at Troy, shrugs his shoulders and with one big kick from the 20 stone six-foot nine-inch-tall monster of a man, the door bursts open. They both walk into the empty and dark house. It's clear nobody has been here for a while with dozens of letters still on the floor mat next to the front door. Little John walks into the kitchen and opens the fridge, pulling a face as the smell hits him straight away.

"Yeah, Chase ain't been here in a while for sure!" John shouts through the kitchen to Troy who is searching the rest of the house for clues on where Chase could be. He comes down from the bedroom holding Chase's passport.

"Well, he ain't left the country..."

Troy says to John holding up the passport. Troy then notices the smell.

"What is that smell John?" He holds his hand up to cover his nose.

"Fridge, he ain't been here in ages Troy" Little John says.

Troy steps away from the kitchen and tells John to open the kitchen window as he walks into the living room of his missing brother. He sits down on the sofa, pondering what could have happened. He is now adamant that Joe has something to do with it.

The next day...

Little John has just phoned one of the Lads for a meet and is driving towards the meeting point.

Joe and April are on their way to East Sussex to view the property Joe has bought.

Little John pulls into the estate the Lads live on and two of them are standing there waiting.

At Chase's house, his brother Troy has made himself at home by getting a couple of his half naked women cleaning the house when one of the girls asks Troy,

"Where do you want your car keys put?" she asks, standing in just a bra and knicker set holding the keys up in her hand.

Troy walks over to her and takes the keys, looking intrigued then goes outside the front door. He points the car key fob at the cars nearby and one car's lights flash and it unlocks. Troy smiles, he now has a ride to get places.

Meanwhile, Little John is talking to the Lads on the estate about something important regarding their friend Jay, plus a job offer.

"I know what happened to Jayson. Meet me at this address tonight, 8pm, don't be late" Little John tells the

185

Lads, who look at each other confused but intrigued with what John has to say.

Joe and April arrive at their new property, a slightly rundown-looking, but very big house. It is also just yards from the beach with the best views you could have. April falls in love with it as soon as she gets out of the car. As they peer through the windows and walk around the back garden, April asks Joe,

"So, when do we get the keys?"

"Within the next few days, just waiting for the paperwork to go through" Joe replies as April follows Joe round looking at the area, smiling at the thought that this will be their new home.

In South London...

Little John phones Troy to go through exactly what he wants the Lads to do, without letting them know Troy is alive. Troy demands that John comes and gets something before he meets the Lads. Troy puts the phone down and picks out a wad of cash from his brother's safe which is behind a photo frame on the wall. He guessed the combination of their mother's date of birth it worked first time popping open the safe containing around £25,000 in cash.

Little John arrives at Chase's house...

Troy tells John that he wants Joe killed and will pay the three Lads a total of £10,000 cash to do it. John will need to be the driver, and no-one is to know it has come from Troy. He hands John £10,000 of the cash he found in his brother's safe. Little John nods as he takes the cash and places it in his inside pocket. Troy then tells him,

"Don't rush John, I can wait a few weeks, just get it done once."

John nods again to agree and goes to leave Troy's house when Troy stops him again.

"Oh, and John, I need clothes from mine" he says, chucking his door keys to Little John who catches the keys and nods unconvincingly before leaving.

11 days later...

MONDAY, OCTOBER 24th 2016...

Joe walks out of a jewellers in Knightsbridge, London.

Ray has finally realised that selling weed is no longer the thing so has stopped selling it and even cut down on smoking it as his job is going well.

Kirsty is in bed unwell, she has been feeling sick the last couple of mornings and is starting to think it may be something else.

April's outfit for the Halloween party in a few days has just arrived, she holds her outfit up against herself and looks in the mirror.

Little John and the Lads have hatched a plan after two of the Lads took the £10,000 deal to kill Joe.

The plan is to shoot Joe with a pistol given to the Lads by Little John and with Halloween only days away, John has hatched the perfect plan.

WEDNESDAY, 26th OCTOBER…

Ray is on his way back from work. Kirsty is at home on the toilet seat holding a pregnancy test waiting for the result. She looks at the test stick confirming she is in fact about 6 weeks pregnant.

"Oh my fucking god!"

"I'm gonna have a baby" Kirsty says to herself still sitting on the toilet in shock.

Joe has been staying in Eastbourne a couple nights a week to work on the house. He has been taking Ray with him on his days off to help finish the house by the sea that Joe bought with all of his savings, and more. With a little more work, Joe has set a deadline to move in by mid-December, at the latest in time for Christmas, about six weeks from now. Joe will then be away clean, living the dream… hopefully.

With Eastbourne to South London being only just over an hour's train journey it isn't long before Ray is home leaving Joe at the house in East Sussex. He walks into the living room. Kirsty is sitting on the sofa still holding the pregnancy test stick in her hand. She is still in shock as she looks at Ray. Ray stops in his tracks, something has happened.

"Babe... what's up?" Ray asks with a worried tone.

Kirsty holds the test stick up, she is now crying.

"I'm pregnant" she says looking at Ray waiting for his response. Ray looks shocked, he pauses to think about what Kirsty has just told him. He then smiles and walks towards Kirsty,

"I'm gonna be a dad" he declares, as Kirsty laughs and cries at the same time.

Less than a mile away...

Troy is driving Chase's tinted windowed car around the manor. It's the first time he has been back around here in months. Troy has not been back home, or close to it, since he got arrested in the underground car park some five months ago. He is driving freely now as it is dark, due to the early winter nights. That along with the tinted windows, means that nobody can see him.

Down in Eastbourne...

Joe is getting himself settled for the night, alone in his soon to be new family home, with a chip shop dinner on a camp bed. He is on his laptop working on his online business, making sure he keeps on top of everything, now needing it more than ever.

Troy has decided to sneak back into his house without anyone seeing him. He parks around the back-alley beside his house. He opens the front door and looks around the place. Walking into the kitchen, he looks at the fridge and goes to open it before pausing. He remembers the smell of Chase's fridge when John opened it, after having been left for months. He thinks twice, stepping away from the fridge and going upstairs to gather some belongings to take back to Chase's. What Little John fetched wasn't enough, or ideal. He grabs a bag of clothes, some jewellery and then pulls out the £15,000 from Chase's safe. He puts most of it in his own safe, keeping a bit back and putting it back in his pocket. He then spies through the window to check the coast is clear before opening the front door slowly. He checks it's all clear again before walking to his car, getting in and driving away, heading back to Chase's

SATURDAY, 29th OCTOBER…

7:14 am…

It's April's birthday…

Joe came home yesterday after working away for a couple of days and it was all going on with the Halloween party and April's birthday. Joe was up early in the morning, leaving April to sleep, and dealing with the kid's breakfast. He tells them,

"Let mummy sleep for a bit on her birthday."

The kids get the presents Joe has bought them to give their mum, along with birthday cards they made at school.

Joe reaches for a small wrapped, boxed present on top of the kitchen cupboard where April wouldn't be able to see or reach it. He walks through the living room telling the kids to come up when the big hand on the clock gets to the six. Allowing about 15 minutes before the kids come up and crash in, Joe creeps upstairs, with his present in one hand and a cup of tea in the other and into the bedroom where April is sleeping. He puts her hot tea on the bedside unit and gently lies beside her. Her eyes open, all sleepy, seeing Joe next to her she hugs him then sees what he has in his hand.

"Happy birthday" Joe says, handing April the small, wrapped present. April unwraps it and opens the box containing a gold necklace.

"Babe!" April yells in shock and joy, she wraps her arms around Joe, kissing him.

Joe pulls the cover off and moves under it, placing his head between April's legs.

"No babe, the kids" April says, with Joe replying,

" We got twelve minutes." This makes April giggle, then grip the cover as Joe hits the spot and gives April another birthday gift. All before Denny and Izzy come up to give their mum her birthday presents and cards.

Ray and Kirsty are in bed having only found out days before that they are expecting a baby. Kirsty rings April to wish her happy birthday and, although it is still early days in the pregnancy, Kirsty wants to tell her best friend the news which is still a secret.

Joe and April's bedroom...

April is gripping the bed headframe with one hand and the other covering her mouth, shaking in climax. Just in time, as Kirsty calls her phone Joe appears from under the cover. April catches her breath with content and, very happy, grabs her phone to answer it to Kirsty.

In Croydon...

Troy is awake, sitting in his brother's living room in his dressing gown deep in thought about what is planned for tonight.

It's Halloween weekend and the main event coincides with April's birthday party taking place tonight at a nearby country club estate which is surrounded by small fields and woodlands.

Back at Joe's...

April is sitting up in bed taking sips of her cup of tea on the phone to Kirsty as Joe gets up and goes to leave the bedroom.

"WHAT?" April yells.

"Joe... Kirsty and Ray are gonna have a baby" April says to Joe now by the bedroom door. He stops and turns back around.

"What?!" Joe replies in shock, then smiling. "I better phone Raymondo" he says, leaving the bedroom.

April then ends the call with Kirsty.

"OK babe, see you a bit later... can't wait" she tells Kirsty before putting the phone down on the bed and says to herself,

"What a morning!"

Just then Denny and Izzy burst through the door screaming,

"HAPPY BIRTHDAY MUMMY"

They jump on her, sitting up in bed with their presents and cards.

A bit later that afternoon...

Little John is with the two Lads on the estate arranging the deal for tonight.

"So, where is the other one?" John asks, talking about the Lad Will.

"He didn't want in. Don't worry, we got this" says Neil.

John thinks about it.

"I don't care how, just don't get caught. and make sure it's Joe...got it?" John demands of both Lads. One pulls the gun out of his pocket, smiling.

"Fucking put it away!"

John says, "Fuck sake", looking around to see if anyone is in sight.

"Just do the job properly and you got ten grand."

He pulls the wad of notes out from his side jacket pocket and the Lads' eyes instantly fix on the cash.

7:15pm...

April is getting ready. The kids are in their Halloween outfits ready for the trick or treaters knocking on the door. April's mum is downstairs in the living room on the sofa watching television as she is staying tonight. With the kids' Nanny there to babysit, April and Joe can celebrate April's birthday at the party until the early hours.

Troy is sitting on his laptop, he has been searching the online social media profiles of Joe, and even April. He has noticed a post highlighting where they will be tonight. With this, Troy rings Little John to tell him, as it is key to know where Joe will be.

Ray and Kirsty turn up at Joe's as all four are sharing a taxi to the venue a few miles away.

As they enter the house Ray, dressed as a vampire, screams. Denny and Izzy scream in fright before giggling and shouting back at Ray,

"Uncle Ray, you scared us!"

Kirsty is following behind Ray smiling, she is dressed as a wicked witch. Joe gives Kirsty a hug and congratulates her on the baby before going upstairs to see April who is still getting ready.

Now that Little John has found out the exact location that Joe will be tonight, he phones the Lads from the estate who plan to shoot Joe.

"Yeah I am going to send you over the address of the place, it's a big area, good for hiding and then getting away quickly." John tells the Lad on the phone.

The Lads are making a new plan of action and set off in a stolen car they just nicked to the country club venue where Joe will be tonight with April, Ray, Kirsty, and other friends.

One Lad is driving and the other is carrying the gun that he will use to shoot Joe.

April is touching up her make-up at her dressing table with Kirsty sitting on the bed. Kirsty is deep in thought.

"Does it hurt?" Kirsty asks about having a baby, looking at April.

April turns to Kirsty.

"Babe, I am not gonna lie, it ain't pretty! But, it's worth it."

"Plus, I'll be there with you all the way" April adds, and Kirsty smiles, reassured.

The Lads Neil and Si arrive at the country club, they drive past slowly and park up in a car park 50 yards up the road. Both the Lads look around, get out of the car, and go for a walk to find a good spot.

Joe, April, Ray, and Kirsty leave the house, leaving Denny and Izzy with April's mum and head to the country club in a booked taxi.

THE COUNTRY CLUB...

Just at the bottom of the beer garden is a small woodland that the Lads have managed to trail to. It is the perfect hiding place in one sense but also very cold. The Lads will have to wait out of sight for their chance to get Joe with a bullet or two.

It's not long after that the taxi arrives, pulling up in the car park. All four friends enter the country club to the sound of the music. A few people are already here.

Back in Croydon...

Troy is relaxing with yet another half-naked girl rubbing him erotically, making up for the time he spent in prison.

Little John is sitting pretty, home alone watching television with his phone beside him waiting for news from the Lads. He picks the phone up and checks it, seemingly slightly anxious about the situation.

The Lads Neil and Si are still in woodlands only 25 feet away from the back entrance and less than six feet from the garden itself. They are now blowing steam, shivering slightly with their tracksuits, black puffer jackets and small woolly hats on, still waiting for the right moment.

Ray and Kirsty, and Joe and April are on the dancefloor when Ray decides he wants a quick cigarette outside. He pulls Joe away from April and heads to the garden leaving April and Kirsty to dance together.

The Lads notice Ray and Joe coming out into the garden, both lighting up cigarettes.

"This is it. This is fucking it!" the Lad Neil with the gun says softly as he reaches for the gun in his pocket and points it in the direction of Joe and Ray.

April and Kirsty are dancing together having a great night for April's birthday on a dance floor with only half a dozen other party goers, when a bullet comes firing through the country club window. The sound of two shots, fired within seconds of each other, causes panic with people screaming. April and Kirsty automatically realise Joe and Ray are outside where the gun shots came from and they both rush to the garden in panic.

The Lad has now fired all three rounds available, with one bullet going through the window of the club. On hearing the gunshots, Ray had instinctively covered Joe and two of the bullets had hit Ray in the back and leg.

Ray falls to the ground with blood showing on his leg and then down his back. His eyes start to close as Joe quickly rings an ambulance while looking around the woodlands trying to see if he sees anyone in the near distance. He notices the Lads running away.

"Yeah, ambulance please" he says, bending down to comfort Ray as his condition gets worse. Just then April and Kirsty get to Joe cradling Ray who is now unconscious in Joe's arms.

Kirsty screams and bends down to try and wake him.

"Ray, babe wake up please! You can't die" Kirsty says, now crying her heart out, placing her hands on Ray's face.

CHAPTER TEN

EVERYBODY'S ON THE RUN

TUESDAY, 1st NOVEMBER...

It is three days after the chaos of Halloween night, which was supposed to be a joyous birthday celebration but ended in Ray getting shot.

Kirsty is sitting beside Ray who has had emergency surgery and been placed in a coma. It is still early days, but one of the bullets ripped through his lung.

Joe is at Rupert's telling him everything, including that he saw the Lads running from the scene. Rupert phones Jag, yet again, telling Joe,

"This geezer has made a good living lately" as he puts the phone to his ear to give Jag another job.

On the estate...

Little John drives onto the estate where the two Lads are waiting for John to pay them for their work. As John gets out of his car, he looks around to make sure the coast is clear. One of the Lads says,

"Fuck me John, where you been? We been trying to call you. You got our money yeah?" he asks John as he walks towards them, towering over them.

"Well, if you got the right person I might of!" John says to the Lad who responds,

"His mate covered him, that's not our fault John" the Lad pleads.

Little John thinks about it and reaches for his inside pocket, pulling out an envelope containing £5000 and hands it to the Lad.

"There is five. If you would of done it properly, you would of got the full ten." John tells the Lad, who is slightly disappointed but takes the envelope of cash.

Joe leaves Rupert's and heads towards his lock up for a tidy up and a think about Ray and everything that is going on.

Troy is also in town again, and again under the darkness of Chase's car's tinted windows.

Joe opens the lock up door, goes in and sits down, totally devastated and done in by it all.

Troy pulls up outside Joe's lock up in Chase's car, he gets out and slowly walks towards the door to Joe's lock up. Joe is inside sitting, pondering in the darkened office room of the lock up. Suddenly a shadow of someone comes towards Joe.

Joe looks up and can't believe what he is seeing.

"Troy?" says Joe with a confused look on his face.

Initially standing in the doorway, Troy walks into the lock up.

"Hello Joe" Troy says looking at Joe with a sarcastic smile, his face then turning serious.

"Hope you did not bet on not seeing me again. Now, where's my money and my brother?" he says walking towards Joe.

Ray is still in a coma in hospital. Kirsty says goodnight to him as she leaves to go home and rest before coming back in the morning.

In the lock up...

Joe tells Troy,

"Your brother did not show up Troy. So what do you want me to do?"

Troy thinks about what Joe says.

"OK what about my money? 60 grand" Troy asks Joe.

Joe pauses for himself to think.

"Well, you gonna have to give me a bit of time. Look Troy, I didn't want to hold your parcel, then it got nicked which I find something wrong about the whole thing" Joe says.

On hearing what Joe says Troy's mood changes, he moves closer to Joe who is still sitting on the chair.

"I don't care what you think Joe, I think you are responsible for my brother's absence, but you say you know nothing... or what about Jay?"

Joe looks at Troy realising now that he knows.

"I tell you what Joe, I will give you one more chance. I want £100,000 or it will be you and your family this time, not your mate." Troy tells Joe, who also now realises that Troy was behind the shooting of Ray, and that it was intended for him, not Ray.

"You got two weeks. John will be in touch" Troy says, turning around and leaving.

He gets in his car and drives back to his own home after being away for so long staying at Chase's. He leaves Joe sitting in his lock up. Joe now has even more to think about than he did when he first came... to think!

Joe pulls out the card with the phone number of the Morris brothers. He looks at the card deep in thought.

The next day...

At the hospital…

Kirsty is sitting beside Ray lying in the hospital bed, he has been in a coma for 4 days now. Ray's eyes start to open and Kirsty feels his hand start to move while she is holding it.

"Oh babe, you're awake" Kirsty says leaning over Ray and touching his face. His eyes open more and he notices where he is. He then looks at Kirsty.

"Did Crystal Palace win?" Ray asks, Kirsty giggles and cries for joy at the same time.

"You and bloody Crystal Palace!"

East Sussex...

Joe is in Eastbourne working on the new house. He is still feeling the shock of seeing Troy again, and now he has to find £100,000 in the next two weeks otherwise Troy will go to war. To be fair, whether he is right or wrong, unfortunately he has a motive.

Joe is touching up bits of paint in both kids' new bedrooms. The kids are helping him, and April is cleaning and making food. Joe has decided it would be safer if April, Denny and Izzy came with him. Even if it means keeping the kids off school rather than them staying at home alone in London, especially now Joe has been targeted.

April's phone starts ringing while she is cooking, she answers it.

"Hey babe" it is Kirsty, who is ringing to tell them about Ray waking up.

"Oh, thank god, how is he?" says April, running upstairs to tell Joe the good news and giving Joe something to smile about at least.

Later that evening...

The Lads Will, Si and Neil are on the estate, the two who shot Ray are boasting to the other one about the new expensive clothes they have bought with the money that Little John gave them for the shooting. Just then Jag drives onto the estate looking for the Lads. He drives past them slowly.

"Boys I don't care bout your clothes, you just wanna make sure this guy don't come for you... coz it's got nothing to do with me"

Will is not impressed about the Lads' antics lately and has been thinking of dropping them out before he gets in trouble for something they, and not him, have done.

There are a few flashes of light along with the sound of three bodies hitting the floor. Jag drives away, all three Lads lie on the cold ground, dying. They have all been shot in a quick second drive-by.

William, struggling for breath, manages to pull his phone out of his pocket to call his mum. She answers her son's call.

"William, William are you there?" Will's mother calls down the phone.

But unfortunately, Will did not get to talk to his mother one last time as he now lies on the ground dead, along with Neil and Si.

13 DAYS LATER...

TUESDAY, 15th NOVEMBER…

Ray is fully recovered and will be leaving the hospital in the next couple of days, going home to pregnant Kirsty.

At Troy's...

Happy to be back in his own castle, sitting on his throne like the king he thinks he is, Troy is planning to start back right where he left off. It's nearly time for Joe to come through with the £100,000 Troy has demanded.

Little John is at home and phones Joe for an update.

"Hello Joe" John says when Joe answers.

"Just checking you aint gonna be late. We wouldn't want that now would we?" John tells Joe.

Joe is still in Eastbourne, finishing off the final bits for the new family home. He tells John,

"Well, I got most of it, just ain't got all of it yet" Joe replies.

"Tomorrow night, East India Docks, 9pm. Come with whatever you have, I am sure Troy will come to a deal" John says, sitting on his sofa.

Joe has no choice but to agree, John puts the phone down. Joe continues to put together their bed, the bedroom being the last room to be finished.

The next day…

The sound of seagulls and the rolling tide of the sea can be heard in the near distance.

Joe and April wake up together in their new bedroom for the first time. They have had to sleep downstairs while Joe finishes everything.

April rolls over and wraps herself around Joe snuggled into the duvet, enjoying the bliss of what it feels like to wake up to this, and that this will be their life from now on.

Joe obviously has other things on his mind and gets up out of bed. April tries to keep him under the warm duvet with her, she locks her arm to his leg. Joe manages to break free. He kisses April and goes to wake the kids.

"Another busy day. Oh, and I need to borrow your car later for a few hours" Joe says to April as he walks out of the bedroom leaving her in bed.

His smile drops as soon as he is out of the room away from April, he is thinking about the meeting he has tonight.

At Troy's...

Troy and Little John are sitting on sofas across from each other about to plan tonight's arrangements. Troy tells the two half naked women sitting on the other sofa to leave the room for a while.

"Go on. Come back in an hour, girls" Troy says as the girls get up and leave the room. Troy then leans over towards John.

"So, we take whatever he brings and then take him out" he tells John, Little John nodding to agree.

Later in the day...

In Eastbourne...

Joe grabs April's car keys from the kitchen side and walks into the living room where April is sitting on the sofa watching the UK snooker Championship on television.

"Alright babe. I'm gonna go grab a few bits from the house and make sure everything is ready for the removals tomorrow. Back in a few hours."

He leans down to kiss April on her forehead, her eyes are fixed to the snooker on television, she replies,

"Be careful please. Love you."

"Love you too" says Joe as he leaves for the front door, on his way to meet Troy via a trip to the lock up to get the kilo of coke. As Joe had said, he didn't have all of the £100,000 but this was what Troy wanted back originally and at the end of the day, it's all Joe has now.

Joe leaves the soon to be new house in Eastbourne, gets in April's car and heads to London.

Troy is getting ready after some time with one of his half naked girls in the bedroom. He waits for the girl to leave before pulling open a drawer and picking up a small gun that he will be taking with him tonight to kill Joe after he takes whatever he has of the £100,000 demanded.

April is still sitting watching the snooker, she checks the time and gets up.

"KIDS, IT'S BEDTIME IN TEN MINUTES" she shouts up the stairs to Denny and Izzy, playing at the kitchen table.

Joe is driving on the motorway, just getting into London.

Troy will be expecting him in less than an hour. Troy and Little John meet up in their cars and both drive towards the docks.

Joe arrives at the lock up. He goes in and opens the safe to get the kilo out and place it back in the bag. He zips the bag up and leaves, turning the lights off before closing and locking the door. Joe gets back in the car, pulls out his phone and makes a call.

Troy and Little John arrive at the dock and park up next to each other in wait for Joe.

In Eastbourne...

April has put Denny to bed and is about to read a bedtime story for Izzy.

At the hospital...

Ray is about to spend his last night in hospital. Kirsty is going to leave to go home and then come and get him tomorrow.

East India Docks, London...

Troy and Little John are waiting in their own separate cars for Joe to turn up. Troy leans over and pulls a small pistol from his glove box. He puts it in his jacket pocket, intending on taking back the bag and then killing Joe in revenge for everything. The lights of a car appear, coming into the docks. Troy pulls his gun and jams it ready before putting it back in his pocket as the car lights get closer.

Eastbourne...

April is lying on Izzy's bed with her, reading her a bedtime story, completely oblivious of what situation Joe is about to be in any second now.

Over at the Docks…

Both Troy and Little John are sitting in their cars only feet away from each other. They get blinded by the oncoming car's full beam headlights.

Flashlights of gunshots are fired with the sound of bullets piercing through metal and glass.

Down in Eastbourne…

April finishes reading the bedtime story, Izzy has fallen asleep in bed. April pulls the duvet up to tuck her in, gently kissing her forehead and creeping out of the bedroom. She turns around to see Izzy fast asleep.

At the docks…

Blinded by the car lights, Little John hears Troy's car get shot to bits, crying, "What the fuck is…"

Bullets fire into Little John who is sitting there helpless in his car.

Smoke from the shootout starts to clear...

Troy and Little John have just been shot to bits while sitting in their car. There are gunshot holes through the windows of both cars, both sit lifeless covered in blood.

20 MINUTES LATER...

Underground car park...

Joe is standing by April's car in the underground car park looking anxious. He paces up and down the side of the car deep in thought when a car drives into the car park, driving towards Joe.

Back at Joe and April's...

April has just finished doing the washing up, she walks into the living room and sits down on the sofa. She picks her phone up, wondering whether to ring Joe to see if he is OK.

Back in London…

The Morris brothers pull up in front of Joe after entering the car park where Joe is waiting for them.

One of the brothers, George, gets out of the car. He walks over to Joe while the other two brothers wait in the car.

'Happy?' he asks Joe, referring to dealing with Troy and Little John.

Joe replies,

"As long as you are happy with the deal?" he enquires, looking down at the bag as he is holding, containing the kilo of cocaine.

George slowly reaches for his inside pocket, Joe looks nervous.

George pulls out an envelope with cash inside.

"£10k for you," says the brother handing the envelope to Joe.

Joe hands the brother the bag in return.

"And a kilo for me. And Troy out of the way for both of us" the brother says before taking the bag and giving Joe a wink of the eye.

"So, he is gone?"

Joe asks, referring to Troy being dead.

George smiles at him with a reassuring face.

"Yeah, both of them."

25 minutes earlier...

East India docks...

The Morris Brothers pull into the docks with the full beam lights on, blinding Troy and Little John who are sitting in their car waiting. All three brothers jump out of the car with automatic machine guns and aim fire, putting dozens of bullets into each car and both Troy and Little John.

George was the last of the brothers to get back in their car. He doused the cars with Troy and Little John in with petrol before setting them alight. They all drove away, leaving Troy and Little John's dead bodies to burn in an inferno in their cars at the dockyards.

Back to the underground car park...

Joe nods his head...

"Cheers"

He thanks George, before George walks back to the car. Just before getting back in, he turns to Joe and says,

"Enjoy the seaside."

He winks at Joe and gets in the car.

Standing in the car park as the Morris brothers drive away, Joe pulls his phone out and phones Rupert.

"Rup, it's sorted mate. It's over.

Rupert in his home studio on the phone to Joe replies,

"All good brother."

With a relieved look on his face, he looks around the room, now at peace.

THE NEXT DAY...

At the Hospital...

Ray has been given the all-clear to go home providing he rests.

Kirsty comes to the hospital to take Ray home. Pushing him out of the hospital in a wheelchair, she helps him into the taxi before taking him home.

In Brixton...

Joe and April pack the last few things from their home into their car. The removal lorry is leaving with all the contents of the home they had lived in for the past ten years.

As they are about to walk out of the door,

"Well, one last look at the place" April says to Joe, looking back through the doorway with a thousand memories of their life in this flat.

She smiles with teary emotion and leaves with Joe to pick up the kids from April's Mum's to take them to their new ho+me in Eastbourne.

A bit later...

Ray is home....

Pregnant Kirsty with her small bump now showing brings a plate of jerk chicken and rice with a drink into the living room where Ray is resting on the sofa. She puts the plate and glass on a small table in front of Ray who is smiling, happy he can eat some real homemade food rather than the hospital shit he has been eating for the last four weeks.

In Eastbourne...

Joe, April and the kids arrived at their new home only a few hours ago and are already unpacking. They are letting the kids decorate the Christmas tree as it is the first one in their new home. Joe is standing on the balcony of their home which overlooks the sea in the distance, he is watching the sunset with a drink in hand. April is inside, among dozens of boxes still to be unpacked, decorating the Christmas tree with the kids, Denny and Izzy. Christmas songs are playing on the radio.

Joe walks in from the balcony and shuts the sliding doors. April comes over to him and they hug each other, looking out of the balcony door window across the sea view. The kids are dancing around the living room with tinsel wrapped around them to the Christmas music playing.

"Did I think Troy was just going to take whatever I had and let me walk free?

Did I fuck!

I've ridden my luck for long enough and who would have thought that the hardest thing would be getting out and away from that bullshit?

Fake banknotes, kilos of cocaine and drug lord gangsters...

Eight people have been shot dead and Ray is lucky to be alive as well as myself.

On to a legitimate online business and a family house by the sea.

2016, what a crazy fucking year!"

~Joe Davies~

Rupert now spends his time in retirement mode,
holidays around the world with Rose when not at home,
safe in his studio doing what he loves.

Billy from Brighton has formed a punk band and is currently gigging around the UK.

"They are actually quite good too!"

Jag now lives in Thailand.

And on the 21st of May 2017, on her 33rd birthday, Kirsty gave birth to a beautiful baby girl. She gave Ray the choice of naming their daughter.

Ray going with the name...

Crystal

Obviously!

THE END

MANY THANKS...

To everyone that has been involved in Pocket in any way, past and present... I cannot show my appreciation enough.

Brixton Streetwear

Unit 57, Brixton village,

London, SW9

brixtonstreetwear.co.uk

Beggars Run

33a Charlotte Road,

London, EC2A

beggarsrun.com

Mickey Mc Cauley   Justin Scriven

Glenn Morris   Eric Mustafa

DJ Jumpin Jack Frost   Pete Bennett

Pete Adams   Daniel O'Connell

Laetitia Leven   Nina Xyda

Charlene Aldridge   Jamel Gabbidon

Andrea Johnson   Laura Nicole

Jag Singh   Gareth Rylatt

Lisa Nash   Mark King

Reuben Blosch   Kirsty Ware

Karen Gomes   Katie Jarvis

Hayden Bowman   John Durrant

Deb, Autumn Olivia, Tom...

and the rest of the band...

'SURRGE'

A special thank you to

Laetitia Leven

Suzy Laver

Sharna Hunt

This was an INDEPENDENT production by...

#ashTag 8ighty2wo productions

#82

hashtag8ighty2wo@gmail.com

D.E.N Productions

Defining Entertainment Naturally

Pocket. Copyright .2021

Made in the USA
Columbia, SC
02 June 2025

58693684R00130